D1241852

AMERICAN ASSHOLE

BACHELOR INTERNATIONAL, BOOK ONE

TARA SUE ME

AFTER SIX PUBLISHING

PROLOGUE

*H*e groaned my name as he pressed deeper inside me and I fisted the white sheets so tightly my knuckles almost matched their color.

We shouldn't be doing this, but more importantly *I* shouldn't be doing this. I should have never let it get this far. I knew better.

I should have never said yes to dinner. I should have never said yes to this trip. I should have never said yes to the contract.

But damn it all I had, even knowing what it would cost us both.

His weight pressed me into the mattress and his breath was hot in my ear. "Are you still with me?" Then for good measure he shifted his hips so his next thrust hit a new spot inside me and I moaned in pleasure.

It seemed I was unable to say no to the man. Nor did I want to. My body moved with his, desperate to draw him deeper.

"Are you?" he asked again, his lips brushing my nape and sending shivers down my spine.

"Yes. Oh, God, yes."

CHAPTER ONE

MIA

I was walking down a sidewalk one day years ago, not really paying attention. My best friend, Wren, was with me and if I had to guess, we were probably talking about boys. It's an assumption we all have that the sidewalk will just be there when we step down. Unknowingly, I made that same assumption, and when my foot came down and met air instead of sidewalk, I sucked in a breath as I tripped into the unseen hole and fell to my knees.

The horrible knowledge that had twisted my stomach upon realizing that what I had counted on to always be there for me and was not, was the same thing I experienced the day my mother died.

She had not been sick. She didn't have anything wrong with her. One minute she and a friend, Opa, were headed to lunch and the next, her car flew into the median as a perfect stranger ran into her at a high speed in his attempt to get away from the pursuing police cruisers. Mom and Opa were killed instantly. The man who hit them had just robbed a gas station. For my entire life, my mother had been my sidewalk and then suddenly, she wasn't there anymore.

Two weeks after her funeral, I had a feeling the sidewalk was going to be ripped out from under me again. I sat in our lawyer's office and I knew it wasn't going to be good news based on the way everyone in the office looked at me when I walked in, eyes filled with something that looked like pity. I hated that. I didn't want their pity.

I also didn't want to be here. Lawyer meetings were about on par with doctor's appointments and they both always had the most uncomfortable waiting areas. It must be a periodical they all subscribe to: *Waiting Rooms to Lose Your Mind In.*

"Clayton," I said, when he finally sat down after his admin gave him some papers he'd asked for. He'd been acting edgy and odd since I walked in."I promise I'm strong enough to handle whatever it is you're hesitant to tell me."

What worried me more than anything at that moment wasn't my suspicion that he was hiding something, but that whatever he had to tell me was going to be much worse than I had originally thought. I had asked a week ago for this meeting and he'd kept postponing with the excuse he didn't have all the paperwork.

"Mia," he said and then stopped as he read something in the folder he'd just received. He looked horrible. He'd always been on the pale side, but he appeared even more so today. Not to mention, his much-too-thin frame didn't help matters out.

"Spit it out, Clayton."

He took his glasses off and though I thought I'd prepared myself for whatever he was going to tell me, I hadn't. Not by a long shot. "You know it's been a rough year for the business," he said.

My mom and I were co-owners of Cross My Heart, a boutique dating agency in downtown Boston. She dealt with the numbers side and the money, while I worked my magic with the people side of the business. We didn't plan to get rich from our venture, but it paid the bills and we were two of the lucky ones who could say we loved our jobs.

Granted, the last year had been more difficult than others, simply because one of our well-known clients had been accused of inappropriately touching a female co-worker. Technically speaking, it shouldn't have affected us at all, but right before the allegations came out, he'd done some promo and advertising for us, so we were seen as guilty by association.

It had unquestionably been a rough time, but mom and I had put our heads together and worked through it. I blinked back a tear. God, I missed her. Who would I weather the next storm with?

"Yes," I told Clayton. I could not fall apart. Not right now. "Mama had told me, but she didn't make it out like it was anything major. In fact, I seem to remember her saying things were looking up recently."

"Yes, well," he said, shuffling through the papers. "The thing is, your mother took a loan and put the business up for collateral."

"What?" I asked, because there was no way he'd just said what I thought he did. "That can't be. There's no way she'd have done something like that and not tell me."

"I'm afraid she did. In fact, I helped with the terms of the deal. I told her when we were doing it that I thought she should bring you in." He shook his head, but refused to look at me. "She didn't want to and I didn't push it the way I should have because she thought she'd be able to repay it without you ever knowing. Obviously, we never expected this."

"How much was the loan for?" My body starting shaking, ever so slightly and I willed myself to stop.

Was that *guilt* I saw reflected in his expression?

"It's not only the matter of the amount, you see," he said. "It's also who the loan was made with."

I was starting to get the feeling that I wasn't *seeing* anything at all. I glared at him. "I think you better explain to me what it is you're so hesitant to talk about."

"Your mother got the loan from Tenor Butler."

He might as well have punched me in the stomach. My mouth opened and closed, but nothing came out. It was several long seconds before I managed to get out two words. "Tenor Butler?"

Oh, my God. Anyone other than him.

Clayton winced. "Yes. She went to a few banks first, but none of them were willing to loan her anything. Tenor was her last hope."

I still couldn't wrap my head around the fact that the business found itself in that much trouble, much less that my mother had to make a deal with the likes of Tenor Butler. But, whatever. I had a bit of money left over from her life insurance. It wasn't a lot, but hopefully it'd be enough to pay Tenor back. "How much did he loan her?"

Yes, there was definitely guilt now, written all over his face. *Shit.*

"I'm so sorry, Mia."

"How much, Clayton?" My heart felt as if it would pound through my chest, because somehow I knew it would be too much for the life insurance to cover. And yet, I still wasn't prepared for his next words.

"Two hundred fifty thousand."

My vision grew blurry and saliva filled my mouth. *God, please don't let me vomit in my lawyer's office.* I placed a hand on my belly in an attempt to stop whatever it was getting ready to do. "A quarter of a million dollars?"

Why? What for the love of God would she need that much money for?

He nodded his confirmation.

There was only one thing that kept me from passing out right there in the chair across from his desk, and that was the knowledge there was no way Mama could have gone through all that money.

"How much of that is available in the business account?" I was an idiot to have to ask. What sort of business owner didn't know how much money they had in the bank? I should have known what our balance was, but Mama was the money person and since her funeral, I'd been purposely putting it off. The thought of seeing her handwriting again and knowing she'd never write anything else...it had been too much. It still felt like too much.

"Umm." He started flipping through the papers on his desk. "Looks like there's about ten thousand as of yesterday morning."

Holy fuck! "You mean to tell me that my mother somehow spent almost a quarter of a million dollars on our business and I didn't have any idea?"

How was that possible? Was I that blind or was she that good at hiding? Following those two questions was the uncomfortable feeling that I didn't know her at all.

"It appears that way."

I stood up even though my legs felt like Jell-O. I placed both of my hands on Clayton's desk and then shoved them in my pockets when I saw how they were shaking, "I can't believe you knew all this and didn't tell me until now." I should be mad at mama, too, but she wasn't here and he was.

"Mia, your mother—"

"Don't give me that bullshit. There was no reason for my mother to get a loan for that much.

Especially from *him*. I don't know what's going on here, but I'll get to the bottom of it eventually and when I do, I plan to find a new attorney."

Unable to be in the same room with him anymore and knowing there was nothing either of us could do to make the situation any better, I spun on my heels and stormed out of his office. I'm sure I received a good number of stares as I made my way out of the office building, but I honestly don't remember.

I'd walked to Clayton's office because it wasn't too far from Cross My Heart and I'd thought the physical activity would be beneficial for me. I supposed in some warped way, it turned out to be just that. Or, if nothing else, it allowed me an acceptable way to work out my anger toward Clayton.

Not that I could actually blame him for everything. Oh, no. That honor belonged to no one other than Tenor Butler himself. Some part of my brain tried to tell the rest of me that logically, the majority of the blame belonged to my mother. But I told that part of my brain to sit down and shut up.

Tenor Butler owned and operated the most successful dating agency in Boston, hell, probably the entire East Coast—Bachelor International. Of course, that wasn't why I didn't like him. Seriously,

I'm not petty enough to be angry because someone is more successful than me.

I didn't like him because I didn't like his entire approach to dating. I'd heard about some of his practices and I thought they were cookie cutter and impersonal. To me, matchmaking was an art. Or at least a skill to master. To Tenor it wasn't anything more than a ten-page questionnaire with multiple choice answers. *Multiple choice.*

Are you kidding me with this?

But he wasn't and obviously, his way worked, because like I said, most successful agency in Boston. And yet, I didn't feel like what he did was real. Anyone could gather statics based on multiple choice answers, but they wouldn't tell you about your client's deep down wants and needs and fears.

Maybe that was it. Maybe I felt as if Tenor was getting ahead by cheating in a way. He'd somehow managed to be successful by circumventing the upfront work needed in order to properly make a match. I let that stew as I walked back.

I thought I'd actually calmed down quite a bit by the time I reached my office. Obviously, though, my countenance left something to be desired because Wren, who'd agreed to sit and watch over the office while I was gone, looked up as soon as I walked in and said, "What the hell happened to you?"

I shook my head. I wasn't really ready to talk about it, wasn't actually sure I'd ever be able to talk about it. But Wren would be the best person to initially talk to because she knew me better than anyone.

I decided to lay it on her all at once. "Mama took a loan out for a quarter of a million dollars."

Wren's jaw dropped open.

"And that's not the worst part," I said.

"No way."

"Yes, way. *Tenor Butler* gave her the loan." It didn't make me sick to my stomach to say it anymore, but my insides still fluttered a little.

Wren's face went unnaturally pale and her eyelashes fluttered for a few seconds. I actually thought she was going to pass out or something, but her color returned and she simply muttered, "Holy shit."

"Right?" I flopped into a nearby chair. Another reason to tell Wren. She knew exactly who Tenor was, so I didn't have to spend time explaining why this was such a horrible thing.

I also truly appreciated that Wren didn't ask me questions I had no answers for, like why Mama needed that much money and where it had all gone. Why the hell Tenor Butler of all people? I'd have to ask those same questions soon enough, but I wasn't ready just yet.

"Tenor Butler," Wren mumbled and then her head shot up and she looked at me with determination in her eyes. "We need to come up with a plan on how you're going to deal with him."

I nodded. A plan was exactly what I needed. "He has to know she passed away."

Of course he would. Any good business person would know such details about someone who owed them money. Especially that much money. He more than likely knew I was her only living relative. I dug my nails into the palm of my hands, not wanting to think about being alone right now.

I couldn't help but wonder if he had any idea at all about what I thought of him and his multiple choice, cookie cutter business. Probably not.

"Yes, and my guess is he's giving you time to grieve before he approaches you," Wren added.

"I'm sure." For some reason that irritated me and I couldn't figure out why. If he'd come by and tried to talk to me the day after her funeral or something, I'd have been justified in my anger toward him. So why was I mad he was giving me space?

"I'll tell you what I'm *not* going to do," I said. "I'm not going to sit here and wait for Mr. High and Mighty Butler to summon me to his chrome and stainless steel high-rise office in the sky."

"What *are* you going to do?"

I smiled. "On Monday morning, bright and early, I'm going to beat him to it. I'm going to show up at his office and insist on seeing him." Today was Friday. That gave me the entire weekend to come up with a plan on what to do once I made it into his office. Surely I could think of something between now and then. Otherwise, I'd be handing all the control over to Tenor and that was not going to happen.

CHAPTER TWO

MIA

*M*onday morning, at a few minutes past nine, I stood in front of the glass and steel skyscraper that housed the office of my nemesis. Why had he chosen that building to run a match making business in? Did his average client feel a greater amount of confidence in such a building as opposed to the office space I was able to afford the rent on that wasn't downtown?

Who knew?

Who cared?

I tried to tell myself I didn't, but I did. Slightly disgusted with myself, I shook my head and walked up the remaining steps. Once inside, I moved out of the flow of traffic headed to the elevator in order to check the directory. Bachelor International shared the twentieth floor with three other companies.

Mama and I had only moved into our current office about three years ago, so I had a general idea of what rental costs were around the Boston area. Bachelor International did extremely well based upon what I knew Tenor had to be shelling out per month for the prestigious address.

After I found my way to the twentieth floor and made my way inside to the reception area, I was pleasantly surprised. The decor was more traditional than sleek contemporary, and instead of the cold and clinical feeling I'd prepared for, the warm woods and muted neutral colors gave off a comforting vibe. All that was lost on me, though. I would never feel comfortable in this place.

An attractive blonde sat at the front desk and gave me a quizzical smile. "Hi, can I help you?"

I walked closer to the desk. "Mia Matthews for Tenor Butler. He's not expecting me. I was hoping he could make some time to see me regardless."

Both her eyebrows went up and her spine went ramrod straight. "Mia Matthews, oh yes." She stood up. "Please excuse me. I'll be right back."

Deciding against sitting down, I remained where I was.

She wasn't gone long at all.

"Mr. Butler said for you to go right on in." She pointed to the door behind her that she'd used seconds before. "He's the last office to your right, at the end of the hall."

"Thank you," I said, feeling somewhat surprised that he'd agreed to see me and also very curious about exactly how many offices were behind the door. I'd assumed he only had a handful of people working for him.

The inner offices of Bachelor International were just as richly appointed as the waiting area and I saw at least five other employees before I made it to the last office on the right.

His door was slightly open and his low, "Come on in, Mia," when I knocked, sent shivers of awareness through my body.

He stood as I entered.

Now, I'd never seen Tenor in person, I'd only seen a few old photographs of him. Mostly back when Mama and I were starting out and we'd researched our competition. I knew he was fine looking, but—*damn*—I didn't expect him to be *that* fine looking.

His messy-yet-still-somehow-beyond-hot hair was a shade somewhere between dark brown and black, and contrasted sharply with the blue in his eyes. His bone structure looked as if he'd been sculpted by a Renaissance master, and the slight scruff at his chin gave him a disheveled appearance that only made him hotter. And his lips? God help me, I wanted those lips all over me. I felt warm all over like he'd turned the heat on and I was actually aware that it had been almost a year since I'd had a man's lips on me.

The lip in question quirked up on one end like it knew I was thinking about it. I lifted my head a little higher and saw his knowing eyes.

Ass.

Unfortunately, my traitorous body didn't care. It still wanted his lips.

He waved to a small sitting area to his right and moved that way to join me. I took a seat in one of the plush leather chairs and he sat down in an identical one next to me.

"I'm so sorry for your loss," he said, all the while looking at me with those captivating eyes. "I can only imagine how tough it's been on you. Your mom and a friend."

"Thank you," I said, pleasantly surprised at how nice he was and that he knew Opa was also a friend of I mine. Why had I always pictured him as a mean, cold-hearted bastard? "Opa was something special. She lived in an assisted living facility. One or both of us would take her to lunch on Wednesdays."

Opa had always looked so forward to our lunches and said they were the highlight of her week. She didn't have any family left. I'd combined her funeral with Mama's. I took a deep breath, not wanting to get upset in front of him.

He tightened his hand into a fist on his knee. "There was a chance you could have also been in that car?"

I shivered. Not for the first time, realizing how close I came to being in the car with them. "Yes and if not for a client who had been running late, I would have been."

"Jesus," he mumbled under his breath.

"I lost my dad ten years ago, and I was an only child, so it's just me now," I blurted out and seconds later I all but clamped my lips shut. I was an emotional train wreck.

Or maybe it was just him.

He nodded. "I'm an only child as well, but I'm very lucky to still have my parents living."

"Are they in Boston?" Did he know how lucky he was?

"Outside New Haven."

"Close enough," I said. The trip to New Haven to where we were took less than three hours.

"And yet, not too close," he said with a sexy, devilish grin that made my heart skip a beat.

Oh, yes, yes, yes. I bet those lips felt incredible. His tongue, too.

I told myself to get a grip and to stop staring at his mouth. I wasn't here to find out anything personal about him, to become his friend, or to learn what he did that he didn't want his parents too close for. I most certainly wasn't here for anything having to do with lips. I was here because he loaned my mother a ton of money. Which meant, I now owed him a quarter of a million dollars.

Shit.

That was enough to wipe the smile off my face and to stop my fantasy of seeing what type of underwear he favored. My gaze dropped to his crotch and then snapped back to his face. I straightened my shoulders. "I'm sure you know why I'm here."

And just like that the Tenor I'd first met disappeared and was replaced by what I knew had to be the hard-ass businessman. "Yes." He straightened his shoulders and his expression became masked. "I was planning to stop by and see you sometime later this week."

"Looks like I beat you to it," I said, matching my posture to his.

"That you did." He smiled, but it wasn't the same as the smile he'd given me before. This one looked cunning. More like what I'd imagined.

"Unfortunately," I said. "I'm not able to pay you back at the moment for what my mother owed you."

The fact was, after spending all weekend studying the books, I wasn't sure if I'd ever be able to repay him. There was no way on God's green Earth I would admit that to him, though.

This obviously didn't come as a surprise to him as he merely nodded at my statement and of course, he already knew. Hell, he probably knew down to the last penny exactly what I had in my bank account. He was a smart businessman and I felt for certain he'd looked into Mom's finances before loaning her the money. Odds were likely he'd looked into mine as well.

Suddenly I felt very exposed sitting next to him. Sort of the way I'd expect to feel if I stood beside him completely naked while he wore all of his clothes. I started feeling all hot and bothered. But thoughts like that were dangerous for many reasons and getting naked in front of Tenor Butler wasn't going to happen.

I turned my head back to him, thankful that he couldn't read minds and hoping that if my cheeks were flushed, he wouldn't ascertain why. It was then I realized he hadn't said anything in response to my statement about not being able to pay him back.

"I mean," I hastened to add, "Don't get me wrong. I will pay you back. I just don't know when."

"I'm not worried about the money," he said, leaning ever so slightly toward me and I couldn't imagine what it was like to not worry about that. "I actually want something very different from money from you."

My head jerked up. Surely he wasn't suggesting.... I tried to look at it subjectively, but could come up nothing other than he wanted sex as payment for the loan. Rage engulfed me and I shot to my feet. "You have some nerve to suggest *that*."

He remained seated and he wrinkled his brows. "Suggest what?"

Seriously? I placed my hands on my hips. "What you were getting ready to suggest."

"What I was getting ready to suggest?" he asked, and he truly looked confused, but then his eyes widened in understanding before narrowing in anger. "Did you think I was going tell you I would forgive the loan if I could fuck you?" he asked as if it was the most ridiculous thought ever.

I crossed my arms. "What else could you possibly mean when you said, 'I want something different from money from you'?"

"That I meant anything other than that." He took a deep breath and ran his fingers through his hair. Somehow the end result made him look even hotter and I hated him in the place of every man who didn't have perfect hair. "I realize I can't simply say you know me better because you don't know me at all."

I raised an eyebrow, still suspicious but feeling a little better.

"However, let me be very clear, I have never traded sexual favors for work, required sex from any of my employees, or dropped the slightest hint of impropriety. And I'm damn well not going to start now. I've worked too hard and too long."

I didn't say anything. I mean, it wasn't like I was going to apologize, because men pulled shit like that all the time. Of course, I may have been jaded thanks to the advertising nightmare Mama and I had dealt with.

"Will you at least sit back down?" His voice calm

once more as he gestured toward the chair I'd vacated.

I sat, but sent him a sharp glance to let him know I wasn't thrilled to be doing so and I didn't have a problem in the world hopping back up if I thought for a second he was heading somewhere I didn't want to go.

"Let me begin a different way," he suggested and I nodded. "We are a large agency and I admit, we don't have the personal touch of other agencies, including your own. In addition, we've received a lot of interest in our international division lately. That in and of itself isn't a problem; we've been promoting it heavily and it *is* in our name. However, in order for it to be as successful as I think it can be, we need to revise our plan. And that's where you come in."

I had been totally with him up to that point, but as soon as he said that was where I came in, I got lost, yet strangely intrigued. "What do you mean?"

"I want you to come work for me."

Tenor Butler wanted me to work for him? I tilted my head and ran his words through my head several times to really let it sink and for me to come up with a halfway intelligent thing to say in response. And as I did, I believed I understood exactly what he was saying. "You want me to close Cross My Heart."

It wasn't a question, so I didn't ask it as one. I merely stated a fact.

"Yes."

I closed my eyes, told myself to think objectively about it. That I couldn't see it as a personal issue, but rather to address it as a business opportunity. This had nothing to do with closing what Mom and I had worked on for so many years. This had everything to do with me looking good and hard at the numbers and realizing he could destroy me with a word.

I raised an eyebrow, still curious in spite of everything. "What's in it for me?"

He gave me a smile that indicated he'd known all along what I'd be asking. He stood and walked over to his desk, took a folder from the top and handed it to me as soon as he returned. "This is a package I created for you. It contains my offer and a few ideas on how I envision you fitting in here. Take some time and look over it. Have your attorneys look over everything." He tapped the folder once with his finger. "Call me if you have any questions. I put my personal number on the top page."

It was a ton of information and obviously not something he did quickly, but rather something he'd given a lot of thought. I didn't quite know what to make of that. How long had he had his eye on me and my agency? I felt uneasy.

I had a lot of reading and thinking ahead of me, but before I could move on, I needed to let him know one thing. "I don't believe in asking my clients multiple choice questions."

"I'm well aware of that, Mia," he said and the hint of playfulness in his tone made me wonder what else he knew about me.

CHAPTER THREE

TENOR

ia left my office and as a result, I'd be worthless the remainder of the day. That was bad, because it wasn't even ten. However, no matter how I looked at it, I had two choices: I could stay in the office and pretend to work or I could admit defeat and leave.

I finally decided to go. I wasn't doing anyone any good and I knew if I stayed in the office, all I'd do was be a distraction to the employees that were working. Sure, I could pretend as if I was just checking up on them, but I'd never been one to micromanage and if I started now, the majority of them would tell me to fuck off. Or at least they'd think it.

Besides, I could always work from home.

I wouldn't, but I could.

I wouldn't be able to concentrate and work no matter where I went today because the truth was, I'd been an asshole and a bastard to Mia. Mia and her mom, Dee, had been on my radar for a long time. They were good at what they did and, as a competitor, I'd kept an eye on them.

I never looked into their finances, but I was always surprised they never quite seemed as successful as I thought they should be. After some time, I came to the conclusion they were doing what they wanted to do and even though I'd manage the business better if it were mine, it wasn't and I should leave them alone.

I'll admit it, a part of me dreamed about having Mia come work for me. I wasn't stupid, after all. Mia was damn good at what she did. She had a personal touch with her clients that I knew my company lacked. Of course, she was hot as fuck, too. Her body was a temptation of soft curves and a sharp mind. Pair that with her deep brown eyes that missed nothing and long dirty blonde hair you could hold onto as you rode her from behind?

If she ended up working for me I'd have to stop visualizing that fantasy.

It wasn't until her mother visited me at my office one day after all the banks had turned her down for a loan that I knew any details about Cross My Heart.

I shouldn't have made the loan. I knew as soon as I heard Dee's pitch that it was stupid to even think about it. But think about it I did. I told her to give me twenty-four hours and I'd give her my answer.

I did enough research into both Dee's personal and business account to know that if I lent her the money, I'd never see it back. I wasn't one to carelessly throw money away, but the truth was, I wouldn't miss it. Not only that, but making the loan would give me something of a connection with Mia.

I looked into Mia's personal finances to see that she was nothing like her mother. I wasn't sure why she let her mother run the numbers part of the business. I doubt it was because she was better at it. Odds were, Mia hated bookkeeping and letting her mom take over freed Mia to do what she liked—making matches. I could hardly blame Mia for that, because she was damn good at it. Her track record proved it, even if her business account did not.

And yet, one thing still bothered me. Why did Dee need so much money? A quarter of a million was more than what they brought in annually. And it was much more than what they needed to run the business. Curious, I ended up digging a little more and wound up knowing all of Dee Matthew's dirty little secrets.

Over the years she had managed to accumulate a lot of debt. And like many people do, she ended up borrowing money to pay back prior loans. After years, it snowballed and she started using business funds for her personal use, but she was good at covering her tracks. I had the impression Mia knew nothing.

In my opinion, what Dee had done was underhanded and dirty. You didn't do things like that and not tell your business parter, much less your own flesh and blood. After Dee's death, I'd feared I'd have to be the one to tell her about the loan. I put off going to see Mia for as long as I could, but eventually it became time for me to suck it up and do it.

I had planned on visiting Mia later in the week, stopping by her office unannounced, but she beat me to it. Her drive was impressive, especially considering how determined she'd had to have been to show up at my office so early.

Yes, I liked Mia a lot and finally talking to her face-to-face only served to further show why. She was more than the matchmaker behind her business, she was also brave and strong. Just talking together for the short amount of time we had was enough for me to see she didn't let anyone push her around.

Although I was still a bit upset her first assumption had been that I would attempt to use the loan to sleep with her. I'd worked hard to have a stellar business reputation. One unmarred and without hints of impropriety. I would have thought my reputation to proceed me, but apparently that was only the case with negative ones.

Even so, the fact remained I wanted her at Bachelor International and I'd do damn near anything to make it happen.

CHAPTER FOUR

MIA

"I need help, Wren," I told her that day at lunch. "Because I'm seriously thinking about taking him up on his offer."

"Of course you are," she said, and I rolled my eyes. "I mean it," she continued, like she didn't know I was mentally flipping her the bird. Trust me. She knew. "You're thinking about it because it's the sensible thing to do, and you're always sensible."

"AKA boring."

"There's nothing boring at looking over all your options before making a decision. That's just smart."

I nodded toward the folder Tenor gave me before I left his office. I'd only had a chance to flip through the pages. "I wish his proposal wasn't as good as I think it's going to be."

"What an odd thing to wish for." Wren shook her head. "Why would you want it to be worse?"

"Because then I could file him away forever in the asshole box and leave him there permanently. It'll be so much harder to do that when I get a chance to read this in detail and realize it's not that cut and dry."

"Little in life is." She thumped my shoulder. "Besides, the world needs fewer assholes, not more."

"I'm fine with fewer assholes, I just like it better when he's one of them." But as soon as I said it, I remembered how hot he was and how genuine he sounded about having me on his team, and I wondered if I really wanted him to be an asshole.

"It makes it easier for you, doesn't it?" she asked with a tilt of her head. "When everyone acts the way you think they should based on the box you have them in?"

"I don't know. You make it sound bad." And it made me *feel* bad.

"You don't like surprises."

I snorted. She got that part right at least. I hated it when things didn't work out the way I had them planned. Or, in the case of Tenor, when people didn't act like I thought they should. It was nicer and things ran better when everything and everyone behaved the way they were supposed to in my mind.

"Which means Tenor should act like an asshole because that's what you've labeled him as," she said and it sounded grossly unfair even to me.

"It sounds even worse when you put it that way," I said.

"Good."

"Good?" I asked. "It's good? What about it is good? And why are you sticking up for him all of a sudden? You know how I feel about him."

"You've judged Tenor based on nothing at all. You've met him all of one time and you'd already made up your mind about him before that. And I'm willing to bet that judgment was made from the fact that you didn't like the way he ran his matchmaking business."

I hated it when Wren was right about me being the asshole. I couldn't deny it. She was right. I'd painted Tenor to be an ass based solely upon the fact that I didn't like the way he ran his business and not on the man himself.

Thinking back to our brief meeting, there hadn't been any part of him that screamed asshole. On the contrary, up until I thought he'd propositioned me with sex, he'd been charming. Talking with him had been rather nice.

Was it possible I'd been wrong about him? Thinking about it made me feel itchy. But the more I thought about it, the more it seemed possible. I glanced at the folder to the side of my plate. The proposal would be very telling.

Wren, of course, could just about read my mind. We'd always been that way with each. Today was no different. She tapped on the folder. "I'm going to leave so you have time to read. Keep an open mind, okay?"

I nodded and stood up to hug her. "Thank you, Wren. I don't know what I'd do without you."

"I'm sure you'd do just fine."

I didn't believe that for a second and I shook my head. "I don't ever want to find out."

She laughed and cocked a hand on her hip. "Lucky for you, I'm not going anywhere. You're stuck with me, sister."

I grinned even though I saw the sadness and truth she kept hidden inside. If she truly had her way, she wouldn't be here in Boston. And she most definitely would not be working as a journalist.

No, for as long as I could remember, Wren only wanted to do one thing and that was dance. She took class after class after class of ballet as we were growing up. She danced before school and she danced after school. She didn't get into the ballet company she wanted, but she didn't let that stop her. She worked teaching classes for kids and filling in when needed anywhere else she could find.

About three years after graduation, she decided to take a few business courses and as it turned out, there were several people from our graduating class at the same school. They would all get together on weekends to party and such. Wren went out with them frequently. She would often beg me to join them, but Mom and I were new business owners and more times than not, I'd turn her down.

I don't regret much in my life, but I do regret that I wasn't there to support Wren during that time. To this day, I'm not sure what exactly happened, but a group of them all went to Italy together and when she came back, she was no longer able to dance due to a skiing accident.

She didn't talk about it then and she still doesn't. I'd learned over the years that it's just one thing I'd have to deal with: not knowing what happened in Italy. I've long since given up trying to get it out of her, but I think there was a man involved.

So, when she looked at me with that sad smile

she tried to hide, and told me I was stuck with her, I smiled back. "We'll say that, but only because we both know it's because I'm never leaving your side."

We said our goodbyes and she went back to not dancing and I picked up the folder Tenor gave me and settled in to read.

Later, when I finally put the pages down, I was surprised because his offer was much later than I'd thought. I glanced at my watch. I'd spent hours going through everything. Because, as I'd just learned, Tenor is nothing if not fastidiously thorough.

The packet he'd put together for me contained not only his offer of employment, but terms and conditions on the forgiveness of the loan, a detailed perspective of Bachelor International, and the bios of all of his current employees, as well as a good number of those no longer with the company.

He noted in the documents that I was free to talk to any of them and ask questions about the job, the company, or him. He'd also indicated that he would pull together information on past clients if I would like to talk with them, but that it would take some time due to confidentiality.

I felt shell-shocked, for lack of a better word. Not only was Tenor nothing even close to an ass, but from all appearances he was hardworking, generous, and honest. In fact, he was so far away from the man I had pictured that I almost wanted to go dig up some dirt on him, just to prove he wasn't perfect.

I pulled out my phone and glanced at the number on the top of the paper. Was it wrong that the way he perfectly wrote his numbers annoyed me? Without allowing myself to think about what I was going to say or ask, I punched the digits of his cell phone into mine.

I told myself it was late and more than likely he was out with friends or on a date or something. He was almost certainly not sitting at home or in his office, waiting for his phone to ring.

Which is why it took me longer than average to respond when he answered with, "Hello?"

"Tenor?" I asked because I still couldn't believe it was him. His voice was just as deep and commanding as I remembered and an unexpected warmth began to grow in my lower belly.

"Yes," he answered and then added, "Is this Mia?"

I closed my eyes in embarrassment. *Damn, the way he said my name.* "Yes. Sorry, I didn't expect you to answer."

He chuckled. "I have to question the type of

people you hang around if they normally don't answer their phone when you call."

"It's not like that," I stopped myself before I blurted out that it was just him I didn't expect to answer. "Besides, you didn't know it was me until I confirmed it."

"True."

"And," I continued. "Now that you know what my number is *and* you made that comment, you'll always have to answer my calls."

"Also true," he said and I heard the smile in his voice. "Although I have to confess, I would have always answered your calls even if I hadn't made that comment. I assure you, it is no hardship."

Was he flirting? I was so stunned I didn't say anything.

Finally, he coughed. "Is there something I can help you with, Mia?"

Right. Right. Right. "I had a chance to read through the proposal."

"Ah, good. Did you have any questions? Anything I can clarify?"

Why do you have to be so nice? But I couldn't ask him that, so I answered with, "Not really. Nothing specific anyway."

The silence between us hummed and I closed

my eyes, as if that would make it go away. But of course it didn't. Why had I called him again?

"Should we get together to discuss everything?" he asked and was it intentional that he used 'get together' instead of 'meet'?

Did I care?

No.

"Yes," I told him. "That would be great."

There was a smile in his voice when he spoke again. "Excellent. I'm in meetings almost all day for the next three days. Are you free for dinner either tomorrow or the next day?"

Dinner? Why dinner? "Umm..." I started and then stopped because I didn't know what else to say.

"I know it's an odd request," he added. "But as I said, I have all-day meetings for the next few days and dinner is the only time I have free. We could always wait until they're all finished, but to be perfectly honest with you, I can be an impatient man when I see something I want."

Two hundred butterflies should not have taken up unexpected residence in my belly at the way his voice grew low and rough as he said that last line. They should not have. This man was a potential employer and I had no business getting butterflies at anything he said.

But I wasn't about to turn him down. I wanted to discuss his proposal and truth be known, I wanted to see if I could get to the bottom of why everything about him affected me the way it did. "Tomorrow night would be perfect."

CHAPTER FIVE

TENOR

The phone call from Mia settled it. I was a bastard and a half. No, on second thought, make that two bastards. I was two bastards with a double helping of lying asshole.

I did *not* have all day meetings for the next three days. There was no reason for me not to have lunch with Mia instead of dinner. Hell, there was no reason for us not to meet at nine-thirty in the morning.

No reason other than I wanted to have dinner with her and I knew as soon as she accepted an offer of employment from me, that door would be closed. Even though I was two bastards with a double helping of lying asshole, I would not in any way, shape, or form, do anything remotely inappropriate with an employee.

"Wrong," my best friend, Piers, said when I told him what I'd done. "You've never done anything inappropriate with an employee *before now*. All bets are off with Mia. You'll rewrite the fucking employee handbook for her."

I almost flipped him the bird, but doing so would only prove him right. Hell, I'd probably brought Mia up every time Piers and I talked since Dee walked into my office.

"I should cancel dinner," I said instead.

"Yes," he said. "As your corporation's attorney, that is my recommendation. However, as your best friend since third grade, I know that isn't going to happen, so instead my advice is, if you're going to fuck her, do it before she officially works for you and don't have her start until this time next month."

"You have got to be the worst lawyer on the planet. I don't know how you managed to pass the bar." Was he actually suggesting I sleep with her for a month and then break it off so she could work for me?

He shrugged. "Truth hurts. That doesn't make me a bad lawyer. It just means I know you too well to think I'd be able to talk you out of having dinner with her tonight."

I stood with a sigh and raked my fingers through my hair as I walked toward the large window in my home office.

I'd worked from home again today, although *work* was a word I'd use lightly. Other than leaving my admin speechless over the fact that I was working from home two days in a row, the only thing remotely resembling work that I'd done was to call Piers over.

I told myself no matter what happened tonight, not that I planned on anything other than dinner happening, tomorrow would be back to normal. I'd wake up and go into the office and everything would be the exact same it always had been. And maybe, just maybe, Bachelor International would have a new employee joining, but that wouldn't change anything.

Because even if something did happen tonight, which it wouldn't, I assured Piers one more time, it would only happen once.

THE HOURS SEEMED to trudge by, but eventually, it

was time to leave for the restaurant. I'd asked Mia if she'd like for me to come by pick her up on my way, but she was quick to remind me that this was a business dinner, not a date, and that no, there was no need for me to do such a thing. She would meet me there.

Because of the way she showed up at my office so unexpectedly, paired with what I'd already knew about her, I fully anticipated her beating me to the restaurant, even though I was a good ten minutes early. However, a quick glance around the entryway showed me I was wrong. I checked in with the hostess, but told her I wanted to wait for the rest of my party before being seated.

When fifteen minutes had passed and Mia was officially late, I began to worry that she wouldn't show up. Hell, she'd have called first wouldn't she? Or was this her not so subtle way of telling me exactly where I could put my job offer?

I pulled my phone out of my pocket and groaned when I realized I'd turned it off after Piers left because he kept texting me smart ass comments. While he seemed to have given up on getting a response out of me, I'd also missed three texts and two phone calls from Mia.

Fuck. I was such an idiot. I pulled up her contact

info so I could call her back, but her line rang a few times and then switched over to voicemail. I didn't want to leave a message. With a sigh I hung up and told myself I had to wait four minutes before calling again. I'd negotiated with myself to wait three and a half when the front door opened and Mia breezed through.

"I saw where you called, but I knew I'd get here faster than it'd take for me to call you back," she said. Other than breathing a bit heavier and quicker than normal, she seemed fine.

"Is everything okay?" I asked. "I'm so sorry. I never turn my phone off, but I did today because my lawyer was being a pain in the ass, and well, since I normally don't turn it off, it didn't register with me to turn it back on."

I was prepared for her to pout or get upset. In my experience, that's what women did when they thought you were ignoring them. Mia, on the other hand, tilted her head slightly and was looking at me with a curious expression.

"What?" I asked.

"Does that work?"

"Does what work?"

"Turning your phone off and ignoring your lawyer," she said. "Because if it does, count me in."

I gave her a tentative smile. It appeared I wasn't going to have to deal with either a pout or an upset woman. "Not really. But in my case, the lawyer in question has been a friend since elementary school, so if I ignore him long enough he just stops by my home and refuses to leave." She nodded, but didn't say anything. "You never answered," I reminded her. "Is everything okay?"

"Oh, yes," she said. "I was just calling to tell you I was going to be a bit late. I went outside to get in my car and I realized I had a flat tire. A nail, of course. I swear, if there's a nail in the road, I'm going to run over it. It's a gift of mine." She glanced down and then looked at me with a mischievous grin. "One call would have been enough, of course, but when you didn't answer, I remembered our earlier conversation and wanted to be obnoxious."

Her response was so unexpected, I laughed. I couldn't help myself. "Thought to teach me a lesson, did you?"

"Yes, but I didn't mean to make you worry. Sorry about that."

I was so happy she wasn't hurt and nothing was wrong, I didn't think twice about being worried. "The only thing that matters is you're fine and you're here." I glanced over to where the hostess of the restaurant waited discreetly. "And, of course, that our table is ready."

She laughed and I held out my hand to her. "Shall we?" I asked.

With a nod, she took my arm and I led her to the front of the restaurant. As we followed the hostess to our table, I couldn't stop myself from watching the woman at my side.

When she arrived a few minutes earlier, I'd been so worried something was wrong, I'd only focused on the fact that she wasn't bleeding and nothing appeared broken. Now, however, I was able to take in all the details that made her, her.

She wore a smart-looking suit in a pale pink that fit and enhanced her figure instead of covering it up completely the way a lot suits did. Her hair was neatly styled and her makeup applied with a light touch. She was beautiful, even though every inch of her screamed that this was one hundred percent a business dinner and not a date, thank you very much, so don't even bother to think otherwise.

Once we were seated, instead of reading the menu, she looked at me. "How were your meetings?"

"My what?" I asked while reading over the specials of the day.

"Your meetings," she said. "The ones that lasted

all day and were the reason why we had to meet tonight for dinner and not lunch."

Oh, damn. *Those* meetings. The completely made up ones I'd obviously forgotten about. "Cancelled," I said, with a smile. "Thank goodness. I hate day-long meetings."

"Cancelled?" The corner of her mouth curled up, just a tad. Almost as if she didn't know if she should believe me or not. Smart woman. "In that case, it must have been a very good day for you."

"Regardless of the meetings," I said. "The day is much better now."

I'd love to say dinner was nice, but dinner was a fucking nightmare. Every damn thing Mia did was a turn on. Not that she did it on purpose. Seriously, people eat with a napkin because sometimes they needed to wipe their mouths. I knew that. More to the fact, I knew Mia was not wiping her mouth in an attempt to turn me on.

That didn't mean my dick understood.

By the time our desserts came, I was in serious trouble. All these years, I'd only given thought to having Mia work for my company and now that it appeared it would finally happen, I had it all wrong. I didn't want her for the company, I wanted her for me. Not as an employee, but as a girlfriend.

Looking as though she was completely content, which I couldn't believe to be the case, she glanced up from the employment contract and gave me a smile before she continued to read. Moments later, she signed it and I should have been happy. Instead, I faked a smile and signed my name under hers.

And with that stroke of the pen, I ensured that the one woman I wanted, I would never have.

CHAPTER SIX

MIA

I couldn't get to sleep that night. I wasn't
sure why, but for some reason I had the
strangest feeling over dinner that Tenor wasn't
happy with me working for Bachelor International.
Although why that would be the case, didn't
make sense.

Seriously, it wasn't my idea of the perfect job and
I wasn't head over heels happy with the situation
myself, but honestly, he was the one who put everything in motion. It made no sense for *him* to be
unhappy with the way things turned out.

More than likely, I was reading the entire situation wrong. Typically, I was nearly almost always
accurate when it came to reading body language, but
I'd be the first to admit that it had been a trying few

months and it made sense for me to be a bit off my game.

After thinking about it more, that had to be what it was. In fact, it made total sense when I stepped back and looked at the situation more objectively. Before we parted ways earlier, Tenor told me he didn't expect me to be at the office until next week. He said he knew it was a difficult time for me and he could see that I was still dealing with my mom's passing.

And what had I done in response to his very nice and very polite offer?

Laughed and said I'd see him in the morning. Although now, I wasn't so sure. Should I call him back and admit I'd thought about it and decided he was right and I'd see him Monday? Or would that make me look too wishy washy?

Damn, I didn't know what to do.

Maybe send him a text? Or would a call be better? He appeared at times to be so easy going and down to earth, I could already tell it might be hard to keep myself in the right frame of mind around him. It was his combination of confidence and good looks. His intelligence and his humor. It set me off my game.

He was my boss and that was that. The sooner I got that through my head, the better.

Like it or not, I was no longer my own boss and the company I worked for belonged to someone else. I was in the process of closing down Cross My Heart and even though it would take time to finalize everything, it felt final to me. The truth of the matter was, I wasn't just in a whole new ballgame, I was playing a different sport altogether.

The best thing I could do was make sure I not only read the rules and knew what they were, but also followed them.

I'd told Tenor I'd be at work tomorrow and that was what was going to happen. No phone call. No text. And no more thinking of him as Tenor. As far as I was concerned, he was Mr. Butler.

I ARRIVED at Bachelor International early the next morning. So early, in fact, I expected to be the first one there. I was shocked, to say the least, when I walked in and saw, Sara, the admin already behind her desk. Makeup completely done. Hair just right. And too free and easy with the smile. God save us all from morning people. At least until the majority of us have had a cup of coffee.

She stood up. "Do you need some help?" Without waiting for me to reply, she took the boxes out of my hand. "To your office?"

"Yes, thank you." I couldn't help but look for Tenor as we walked down the hallway. But the entire office was silent.

Sara put the boxes on the spot I indicated, but appeared to be in no hurry to return to her desk. "Can I help with anything else?"

"No. I've got the rest of it. Thank you so much for carrying the boxes to my office. If you hadn't been here, I'd have probably dropped at least one of them on my toe." I peeked outside and into the empty hall. "What time do people usually get here?"

"Most arrive before nine, but Mr. Butler is almost always here by seven-thirty."

In fifteen minutes, then. Maybe he'd be happier today.

He would stop by my office, wouldn't he? Being polite and all? Swing by to say hello and welcome to his newest employee?

How great would it be if I already had my area set up?

So great, I decided. I grinned and went to work.

An hour later, I'd met six other employees and most were shocked to see me. Obviously, Tenor hadn't told everyone I would be working for him and I wasn't sure how I felt about that. At first, I was a bit hurt. After all, I had been a direct competitor and now I was one of his employees. Wouldn't that naturally be something you'd bring up?

"You know that badass matcher, Mia? She works here now."

But then, maybe it made sense that he hadn't told everyone. Because they'd want to know why and how would he answer?

"Her mom owed me a quarter of a million dollars."

Yeah, on second thought, it was a good thing he hadn't told everyone.

But even if that had been the case, I couldn't come up with any reasons why he wouldn't stop by or at least pop his head in my office to say hello. I tried to convince myself that he hadn't made it to the office yet. Traffic was bad or perhaps he was sick. But no, I heard his voice as he walked down the hall. He was in the office today; he just didn't want to talk to me.

And why should he? I asked myself as the truth hit me. He'd gotten exactly what he wanted. I was working for him and my agency had closed down. Why bother being nice to me anymore? I could have kicked myself for letting my guard down any at all where he was concerned.

My initial assessment had been the correct one. He was an asshole who would stop at nothing to get what he wanted. Actually, the more I thought about it, he was even worse than I'd originally thought. Because he'd led me to believe there was a good guy under that gruff exterior and the truth was, there wasn't.

I tapped my pen on the top of my desk. This wasn't over, not by a long shot. I'd concede the battle to Tenor, but I had all intentions of winning the war.

CHAPTER SEVEN

I didn't stop by to see Mia until near the end of her first day in the office. It was a dick move on my part and I knew it, but all day I kept thinking about how well we were getting along until she signed the employment contract. I couldn't get the thought out of my head that hiring her had been a bad decision. I was too attracted to her and since I couldn't do anything about it, avoidance seemed the best way to go.

My opinion on hiring her didn't change very much seeing her sitting in an office that I owned. Yes, I decided. I'd fucked up and fucked up bad. Her back was to the door because she wasn't sitting at her desk, but standing and facing a back wall. After a second or two, I realized that she was hanging pictures.

"Do you need help?" I asked, coming through the door.

Unfortunately, I startled her and she somehow managed to hit her finger with the hammer instead of the nail.

"Ow! Shit!" She shook her hand while glaring at me, and then she stuck her thumb in her mouth. "What?" She asked around her thumb.

Good lord, the sight of her thumb in her mouth and every thought in my head left until the only things I could think about were her mouth, my dick, and introducing the two of them. "I stopped by to see how you were doing, saw you and asked if you needed help."

She pulled her thumb out of her mouth with a *pop. Fucking hell.* "As you can see," she said with a wave of her hand. Everything about her was cold, even her voice was frosty. "I managed to hang three others without your help and was doing perfectly fine with the fourth until you came by."

It had been wrong of me to not stop by earlier in the day to see and speak with her. Whatever camaraderie we had managed to achieve the day before, I'd shot straight to hell in less than twenty hours.

In some hard-to-imagine universe, I supposed it could be seen as a good thing. From the expression on her face, I couldn't see her ever agreeing to dinner again. Flirting looked just about as improbable.

And yet...

I still felt the same. Whatever her feelings for me were, they had not changed mine for her. I wanted her. "I should have been by earlier and helped you with the other three," I said.

"What?" She still held a hammer in her hand, I noted with a bit of unease. "Why would it ever occur to you to stop by and help me hang pictures? How could that thought cross your mind when you couldn't even stop by my office to say good morning, so glad to have you here, or screw you, on the way to your own office? Which, I might add, is no more than ten steps from here."

A quick glance at her desk showed Sara had given her our policy books to read. But yes, not stopping by earlier was clearly a mistake. That, at least, was now perfectly clear. It hit me at that moment, I could lie and make up a story about having a meeting. No doubt, she'd see straight through that since I'd already used it once before. Or, option two, I could tell her the truth.

But as I stood there looking at her, I couldn't see

her taking it well that I had feelings for her and that I was questioning my decision to bring her onboard. So, I went with option three, landing somewhere between options one and two.

"I agree I should have made it a point to stop by sooner. In fact, I'd planned to do that very thing. But as I walked into the building today, I also knew it'd be your first day working for someone else. I wasn't sure you wanted to see me." It wasn't a complete lie. I had thought that as I entered the building, but it hadn't been the deciding factor for me.

Regardless of that fact, her expression had lost some if its ire and she watched me with slightly less anger. Heavy emphasis on the *slightly*.

She placed the hammer on her desk. "What exactly are you saying?"

"Please forgive me for being completely clueless. I'd say it wouldn't happen again, but I'm sure it will and I don't want to lie."

More of her anger fell away. "Okay," she said. "You're forgiven. But only this once. Don't take this as precedence."

"Duly noted." I nodded toward the unhung picture, still on the floor where she'd left it after hitting her thumb with the hammer. "Now can I help you with the fourth?"

She took a deep breath and sighed. "I don't know. Now I'm thinking maybe this space only needs three. Do you think it needs another one?"

"Seriously? You're asking me for decorating advice?" Because I sucked at decorating.

"This place doesn't look so bad."

It didn't and there was a reason why that was the case. "I know what my strengths and weaknesses are. Trust me, decorating is one hundred percent weakness. I hired a decorator for the office, my place here in Boston, and my vacation home on Hawaii's Big Island." I added that last one just to get a reaction. Another dick move. Apparently, those were all I was capable of today.

Her eyes widened. "You have a vacation home in Hawaii?"

"Yes, and it's beautiful."

She didn't say anything, rather, she stood there looking at me with her arms crossed and her head titled to one side. I felt as if I was a science experiment.

"What?" I finally asked.

Her lips lifted into somewhat of a smile and I relaxed a bit. "I just realized that whatever I was charging for my services before weren't nearly enough. It never occurred to me that I might possibly be able to afford a vacation home one day. In Hawaii, no less." She stopped and thought for a moment before asking, "You know what that means don't you?"

"No." Honestly, I had no idea since I was focused on her mouth.

"I should have made you pay me more."

I loved how she could deliver a line like that so deadpan and I couldn't tell if she was joking or not. "Now you know," I told her.

She bent down to pick up the fourth picture and placed it on her desk. "I don't think I'm going to hang this one. Three are good enough for now and I can always either add the fourth one later or rotate which ones I have up."

"Works for me." I shrugged. "Like I said, I don't decorate." I looked at my watch and it was well after time I left. Mia obviously thought the same because she started packing up her desk. "Did you park in the deck?" I asked her and at her nod, I continued. "Walk out with me?"

"Has everyone else gone home?"

"Usually by this time, there are only a few people still here." I raised an eyebrow. "Are you worried about being seen with me?"

"I'm new and it's bad enough I used to own a

competing business. Don't make it worse by making me look like the boss's favorite."

"And walking out with your boss, who just so happened to be leaving at the same time you were, will give people reason to think that?"

She picked up her purse.

"Mia," I said as calmly as I could. "If I hear so much as a whisper about anyone talking about you, that person will be looking for a new job."

"You can't fire someone just because they were talking about me."

"Watch me," I told her as we walked out of the office. I nodded to Sara as we passed. "This is a private company. I don't answer to shareholders. I can pretty much do anything I want and get away with it." It sounded smug and prideful, but it was the truth.

I waited for her to say something else, but she was silent as we made it into the parking deck.

We parted ways at the elevator. I had to walk down a flight of stairs to get to my car and she'd parked on the fifth level. I waited for the elevator with her. I knew it was a safe place, but you could never be too careful.

"I hope you had a good first day, Mia," I said as the doors closed behind her.

CHAPTER EIGHT

MIA

"*G*entleman might prefer blondes, but women prefer assholes."

Wren rolled her eyes at me, but kept silent.

"Come on," I said, watching people go past our table as we finished eating our favorite dairy-free ice cream. It was a beautiful Boston afternoon and we were celebrating the end of my first day. "You know it's true."

"Even if it is true, and I'm not saying it is," she said. "It doesn't make sense."

"It doesn't have to make sense for it to be true. Seriously, if you really think about it, a lot of things that are true don't make sense. But research has shown that after interacting with two men, *generally speaking*, the woman is usually more attracted to the asshole."

Wren took a big bite of her peanut butter chocolate cookie ice cream and hummed her delight before turning her attention back to me. "I can't believe someone did research on that."

I shrugged. "Can't argue with science."

"And as a matchmaker, whose job it is to find your clients that one true love, their soulmate, what do you think of that study?"

"Skeptical at first, but now I believe it, completely."

She raised an eyebrow. "It wasn't your study, was it?"

We both shared a laugh over the idea of me running a study.

"No, but seriously," I said, when we could both speak again. "You should write this down. Use it for your next big investigative piece."

"An in-depth look into the dating habits of assholes?"

"Hey," I said with a grin. "Beats what you normally find in the newspaper."

She sucked the last bit of ice cream off her spoon. "True that."

"The way I see it, we're all assholes. Just of

varying degrees. As a matchmaker, it's my job to find the one you're most compatible with." I couldn't help but wonder if Tenor had ever taken his company's multiple choice assessment.

"This doesn't explain to me why women pass on the nice guy in favor of the dickwad."

"I don't think dickwad and asshole are interchangeable terms, but I'll ignore that for right now." I also ignored her smart comment in response to my statement. "Look at it this way, when you think of your perfect man, he's not really perfect, is he? Even if he always holds the door open for you and helps old ladies cross the street, you want him to be a little bad, right?"

I could tell she was starting to see things my way when she got that far away look in her eyes.

I dropped my voice. "A nice guy wouldn't spank your ass while taking you from the back or push you against a wall because he had to fuck you right now, this second, would he?"

"No," she answered, even though I'd meant for it to be a rhetorical question and had actually been picturing Tenor pushing me against a wall.

"But a mostly good guy with a dash of asshole?"

"For sure yes."

"Now do you see what I was I saying?" I couldn't

help the fact that my question came out a bit smug. At her nod in response to my question, I asked, "And what is the takeaway from all this?"

"Assholes are inevitable," she mused. "Might as well use them for sex and get something out of them."

I almost snorted water out of my nose. "I don't think that came out the way you intended."

"It made more sense in my head," she said, flushing a bit. "And didn't sound so perverted."

"Please," I said with a wave of my hand. "Perverted thoughts are the best kind."

"Says the matchmaker for assholes."

"Someone has to do it."

Her expression grew serious. "How are you doing with the business?"

"It gets easier everyday. Just ready to finalize everything and be done with it, you know?" I asked, because I knew she meant my old business and not my new job.

She took my hand and gave it a squeeze. "I know." The smile slowly returned to her face. "Let's go for a walk. We'll see if we can find the biggest asshole in Boston and convince him to let you find his soulmate."

"I know who the biggest asshole in Boston is."

But I stood up and threw my trash away. "I work for him. Don't you remember?"

"Hard not to, with you talking about him all the time."

"I do not talk about him all the time." *Maybe half the time, but not all.*

She just snorted, but kept walking.

"Do I?" I asked, but there was no response.

As LOATHE as I was to admit it, working at Bachelor International was not too bad. Certainly, it was better than I had anticipated. The other employees were friendly and Tenor stayed out of my way.

I had spent my first two weeks in an orientation and training type of atmosphere. I thought the training was a bit beneath me, to be honest. I mean, I had run my own business doing the same exact thing, but Tenor refused to budge. He insisted everyone have the exact same training so there would be no foreseeable way for the new hire not be told something.

Frankly, I thought it was a colossal waste of time and had no trouble telling him as much the few times he dropped by my office to see how I was doing. He refused to allow me to skip anything, however, so at the end of two weeks, I'd yet to be given my own clients, much less been told anything beyond the high level details of the international division.

The other time suck Tenor stood by were staff meetings. Every other day, he gathered all the employees together at nine. *Every other day.* When the woman who had the office next to mine, Rebecca, told me that, I'd laughed because I thought she was joking. My laughter soon died when I noticed she wasn't laughing with me.

"You aren't joking," I said.

Not only was she not joking, she said Tenor felt very strongly about these meetings and you didn't miss them unless you were in the hospital. I rolled my eyes because I thought that was overkill if I'd ever heard it, but I parked my butt in the conference chair at five minutes before nine every other day. Every Monday, Wednesday, and Friday.

The Friday of my two-week anniversary was no different. I took my seat and Tenor glanced my way and gave me a wink and a smile. I thought the wink was a bit much, but maybe he was trying to tell me he was keeping an eye on me and not to nod off like I had on Wednesday.

As always, I was bored out of my mind and by

the time we were halfway through, I was snoozing or at least attempting to sleep with my eyes open. I'd given up any pretense of interest at all. In fact, I was trying to decide if I could block out the second half while still sitting in the room when I noticed that everyone was looking at me.

Fucking hell, had someone mentioned me? I turned back to Tenor, but he was watching me with a very amused expression.

"Can you repeat the question?" I asked him.

The corner of his mouth lifted in somewhat of a smile, but I had the feeling it wasn't a question I'd missed. No, based on the way everyone around the table smirked, I'd missed something much, much bigger than a question.

"I was talking about the potential for expansion in other cities," he said.

I nodded. At dinner the night I'd signed the contract agreeing to work for him, he'd touched on expanding the business. He'd sounded very excited talking about it and all the while, I was trying to wrap my head around a matchmaking company being a franchise. I had never even considered doing anything like that. Either way, I hadn't expected it to come up again so soon.

"I had a call yesterday morning from a colleague

in Atlanta," he said. "He's heard that the owner of The One For You Agency is thinking about selling. He's set up a meeting for the beginning of next week."

Again I nodded, but didn't understand how this in anyway involved me. I mean, seriously, did he have to stop the entire meeting and repeat himself simply because I'd been daydreaming?

I needed more caffeine. Unfortunately, there was not enough coffee in the world.

"I was informing the group that I was going to ask you to travel with me to Atlanta, since you recently sold your own business and joined us," he said as if it was nothing at all. "I'll stop your office after lunch so we can discuss in further detail."

I only nodded, why he hadn't stopped by my office before the meeting? Wouldn't it make more sense to do it that way than to spring it on me at a staff meeting?

Unless he knew that because I was relatively new, I wouldn't question him in front of everyone. Perhaps he'd planned it to happen just that way. He'd smoothly *by the way* bring up in the staff meeting that he would be going to Atlanta and just *so you know*, I'll be taking the new chick with me. Knowing, of course, the new chick wouldn't say anything and when he stopped by her office after lunch, she'd agree because what else could she do?

I narrowed my eyes at Tenor as he closed the meeting. He thought he had me right where he wanted me. And maybe he did. At least for now, anyway. But I was onto him and I was going to keep my eye on him very closely.

OF COURSE he was nothing but smiles when he stopped by my office after lunch. I'd finished a peanut butter sandwich at my desk and had just cleared the crumbs into the trashcan when he knocked on my half-opened door.

"Knock. Knock," he said, entering with a grin.

Damn, he was much too handsome. I swore sometimes it hurt he looked so good. Especially dressed the way he was today. I'd been too bored and later distracted to take note of it during the staff meeting, but now...

The way he strolled into the room as though he owed it.

He does, I whispered in my head.

When paired with the suit I knew had to be

custom and made from a blue material that somehow matched his eyes just right?

Oh, yes. I had a feeling Tenor Butler knew exactly what he was doing and that confidence shook me as much as it turned me on.

"Did you have a nice lunch?" I asked.

"Yes, thanks." He pulled one of the chairs across from me close so he could place some papers on top of my desk. I noticed his fingers. Funny how I didn't remember seeing them before even though I knew I had.

But I didn't see how it could be possible for me to have seen them and not remembered. His fingers were so long and even though I knew he had a desk job, they didn't strike me as idle fingers. They moved with a purpose. The way I assumed his entire body did and suddenly, I wanted to touch those fingers and have them touch me in return.

"Mia?" he asked.

"Huh?" But I was still looking at his fingers while at the same time calling myself an idiot for doing so.

"Are you okay? You seem to have drifted for a minute there."

Several minutes actually, but I wasn't about to admit that. Nor would I ever tell him what I'd been thinking. I nodded.

"I wanted to apologize for springing the Atlanta trip on you the way I did."

He came into my office a lot to apologize about one thing or another. I wondered if he realized that or if he even cared. I got the impression, although I could be mistaken, that he wasn't one to apologize often. Of course, I was pretty sure that had more to do with the fact that he was rarely wrong as opposed to not being one to admit when he was.

"No need to apologize," I told him. "I should have been paying closer attention during the staff meeting instead of daydreaming the way I was."

"Is it a problem for you to travel to Atlanta? If it is, you don't have to go. It was wrong for me to do go about it the way I did." He glanced across the desk and met my eyes. "But I have to be honest with you, Mia. I do want you to go to Atlanta with me and I would very much like your impression of the business we'll be discussing."

I was positive I wasn't able to school my expression quick enough, but I didn't feel assured enough in his presence to question him.

"It surprises you that I want your opinion?" he asked. "Why?"

"Why would you care about what I think? What about me makes me so special that you would want me to travel with you? I'm nobody. I'm a has been business owner who lost her business because she didn't know enough about what her partner was doing."

He closed his eyes and I got the feeling that I had touched on a sensitive subject for him. But why?

"I should never have made the loan with Dee," he whispered. "Not without knowing you were totally onboard and knew about the entire deal."

Was that what put the guilty look on his face? I found that hard to believe. It didn't fit in with the badass business man I thought he was.

Though I wasn't sure if that said more about him or me.

And it didn't escape my attention that he never actually answered my original question. But instead of bringing that up, I decided to continue with his line of conversation. "It wasn't your fault I didn't know and I can hardly blame you for that. That's all on Mama. Not you."

"Thank you for saying that, I appreciate it. But I'm not at that point yet. I'm not a completely good guy, you know."

He was looking at me all playful like. "Oh, I never said you were," I said matching his style. "I'm sure there are many things you should apologize for; that deal just isn't one of them."

For a second, it appeared as if he didn't know if I was being serious or not. To be honest, I wasn't completely sure myself. But then he smiled and broke into a laugh and I found myself joining in.

CHAPTER NINE

TENOR

I decided we should leave for Atlanta on Sunday afternoon instead of Monday morning the way I had originally planned. If there was one thing I hated, it was flying out on the same day as a meeting. Experience had taught me when you did, you might as well beg for a delay because nine times out of ten that was what would happen.

I called Mia on Saturday morning and she didn't sound as if she cared when we left. We would fly back home on Tuesday. Since she didn't have a company credit card yet, I told her I'd pay for everything, but that if I didn't happen to be around, she could expense it. That seemed to surprise her, but I couldn't figure out why.

We flew out late Sunday afternoon. It was the

first time I'd ever seen her in anything casual. I'd thought she looked hot dressed up for dinner the night she agreed to come work for me. But seeing her in a pair of worn jeans and a tee shirt that looked silky soft, she looked just as amazing.

"Thanks for agreeing to fly out early," I told her as we waited for our flight to board. "I don't like flying in the day of a meeting."

"It's no bother," she said. "But if that's the case, why didn't you book us on Sunday flights to begin with?"

"I didn't book them initially. I had Sara do it. I didn't even see the arrangements she'd made until I got home on Friday night."

She nodded and at that moment we are called to board. Once we were seated, we started talking about Atlanta. She'd never been, but had always wanted to. I told her we used to vacation in Georgia near Saint Simmons Island. For the rest of the flight we chatted non-stop.

It was refreshing talking with Mia. Unlike the women I went out with, she didn't try to be anyone or anything she wasn't. She was just Mia and you could either take her or leave her. She didn't seem to care which.

I wanted to take her.

Repeatedly.

But I couldn't because I was her boss. I could, however, take her out for a nice dinner and I had every intention of doing so. I planned to ask her as soon as we checked in and before we headed to our rooms.

We were standing in line to do just that and I was getting a bit impatient. Apparently, there was some sort of convention or something taking place at the hotel and a lot of the attendees were checking in at the same time we were.

Finally, the guy in front of us stepped up and we were next in line.

"Thank goodness," I said. "There for a minute I was afraid we'd be in line until tomorrow and flying in early wouldn't have done us any good."

She chuckled at my weak attempt at humor and I was pleased to have gotten a reaction out of her.

"Mia?" Someone off to our side asked.

We both turned to see who it was. Mia squealed. Then she let go of her bag and ran to the guy, throwing her arms around him.

"Oh my, God, Benjamin Douglas!" She nearly yelled.

"Wow, Mia," he said when she stepped away. "How long has it been?"

"Four or five years, I'm sure."

I could say I watched them, but the truth was I studied them. Looking for any clues in their body language to tell me if they were old lovers or merely friends. I was leaning toward lover, but I really didn't have anything concrete to base that on. Either way, what were the odds of Mia running into someone she knew in *Atlanta*?

"Sir?" the lady at the front desk said.

I waved Mia away when she took a step toward me. "I've got this. Don't worry."

I did my best not to be distracted or try and eavesdrop on their conversation. Once I'd secured our rooms and got us checked in, I walked to where the two of them were talking, bringing Mia's bag with me.

"Tenor," she said, her eyes sparkling. "This is Benjamin Douglas. We went to college together and he's here for the cyber security conference. Benjamin, this is Tenor Butler. My boss."

Benjamin and I shook hands and lied about how nice it was meet each other. Yes, they had definitely been lovers, I could tell now. It was something in the way he looked at her. Like he had some sort of personal or secret knowledge about her that he knew I didn't have.

"If you don't have dinner plans tonight, Mia," he said, shutting me out of the conversation entirely. "I'd love to take you somewhere to catch up."

Mia's eyes grew wide with excitement but all at once she sighed and dropped her shoulders. "I'd love to, but I can't leave Tenor alone."

By the way Benjamin glared at me, it was clear he wouldn't care if I fell off the face of the Earth and never came back. I purposely chose not to pay him any attention, deciding instead to focus on Mia. It was obvious she wanted to go with him, but if I asked her, she'd stay with me.

As much as I wanted her, I wanted the feeling to be mutual, and if she stayed and had dinner with me, it would be out of duty. I couldn't do that. I was going to be the bigger person and I would let her go.

I shot them both a smile I didn't feel and lied. "Yes, you can. You two haven't seen each other in years, there's no way I'm going to stand in the way of that. I'm a big boy, I can do dinner alone. Besides." I gave a fake yawn. "I'm really tired and I was thinking of turning in early anyway."

"Are you sure?" Mia asked, raising an eyebrow just a touch.

"Absolutely." Because what difference would one more lie make?

"Mia," Benjamin said. "Why don't you go drop your things in your room and meet me back down here in about forty-five minutes?"

Mia beamed at him. Fucking beamed. "That would be great. It'll give me time to freshen up. I don't know why traveling always makes me feel so dirty."

She couldn't have meant for it to sound hot, but somehow it did. Benjamin obviously thought so too, I saw the way he tried to shift himself without anyone noticing. But I noticed and if I hadn't already decided I didn't like the man, that would have done it.

He smiled at her. "I'll see you in forty-five."

She didn't move, so I held out her room key. "Mia, here's your key. I'll get the elevator."

"What?" She blinked a few times. "Right. My key. See you in a few, Benjamin."

I turned toward the center of the lobby to where the elevators were located. Once again feeling the press of the crowd around me. What were the odds that with all the people present for the conference, that the date of the conference just happened to occur on the same day that we took an unplanned trip to Atlanta, and that Mia and Benjamin would run into each other in the hotel lobby?

"Wow," Mia said as we piled into an elevator with a horde of people. "Talk about your small world. I can't believe I ran into Benjamin. It's been years."

I knew that, of course, since I'd been standing right there when it happened. It wasn't like I needed a replay. But I didn't say anything of the sort. I shook my head and muttered something about a small world.

We were staying on the twenty-fifth floor out of thirty and if we didn't stop at every floor on the way up to our room, it certainly felt like we did.

"Are you sure you don't mind?" She asked somewhere around the eighteenth floor.

"I'm sure. You go have a wonderful evening catching up with your old friend. I'm going to order room service and call it a night." The elevator stopped on the twenty-second floor and we were the only ones still on. "Let's meet for breakfast tomorrow in the restaurant downstairs around seven-thirty."

She nodded and the elevator stopped on our floor. When Sara booked our rooms, she asked for them to be close together and adjoining if possible. Of course that meant Mia was in the room right next to mine. And of course, I could hear her door close as she stepped inside. Which meant I'd be able to hear what time she got in later that night.

Because I knew I wouldn't stop listening until she was safely back inside.

It wasn't until about an hour later it hit me: what if she brought him back to her room?

I didn't allow myself to dwell on the fact that Mia was out with an ex-lover who appeared to be much too interested in reconnecting and reigniting their past. I was her boss, her employer, the man who signed her check, and as such, I had no business even thinking about her love life or who she had dinner with. It had nothing to do with our relationship. Nothing.

Yet, it didn't matter how many times I repeated that to myself, I wasn't able to get my mind to accept it.

I eventually ordered room service the way I told her I would. I tried to pretend it was because I was really tired but I wasn't. The real reason was I didn't want to leave the room. And also because I secretly hoped Mia's date was horribly awful and she'd run out of wherever he took her. Instead of going to her room, she'd knock on my door. I'd let her in and we'd walk to the couch. I would be quiet and let her take charge of the conversation.

In my mind, I planned it all out. Eventually, she'd tell me what happened. I wasn't sure exactly. Sometimes I made Benjamin an utter and complete ass from the very beginning. But as much enjoyment as I got out of those scenarios, I didn't head in that direction the majority of the time because I didn't think Benjamin would act that way. Nothing on him but more to the fact I didn't think Mia would be attracted to a man like that.

I'm honestly not sure how many different paths I went down trying to picture how Mia's date was going. In retrospect, I knew it wasn't a healthy way to spend my time. But then again, I was holed up in my hotel room, basically stalking my employee in an effort to eavesdrop on her date. So yeah, healthy wasn't on the menu.

I jerked awake at the sound of the door to her room opening. I sat up and looked at the clock. Half past midnight. What the fuck? Where had she been so long and when had I fallen asleep? I didn't move from my spot on the couch though because it was the best place for me to hear if someone was with her.

Was he?

"Are you sure I can't talk you into staying with me tonight?"

Fucking, Benjamin.

"No," Mia said and her voice was stern and almost angry with maybe a hint of fear. "I've already said no and I let you walk me to my room, so now I think it's time for you to leave."

I jumped to my feet. I'd never heard Mia use that tone of voice. I wasn't sure what was happening but it didn't sound right. Something was definitely off.

"Now, Mia, don't be like that. Come on over here and give me a kiss."

"I've already said no." Mia's voice definitely held a hint of fear and I was halfway across the floor when he spoke again.

"But if you'll agree to one kiss, I bet I can get you to change your mind on sharing my room."

"Benjamin. Leave."

He may have answered her. I wasn't sure. By that time, listening was the very last thing on my mind. The only thing I cared about was getting him away from her. It took a matter of seconds before I was out of my room and in hers.

I didn't spare more than a fleeting thought that neither one of them had locked the door, because as I burst into her room, he had her backed against the couch and he was towering over her.

That was all it took. He had his fucking hands on her after she'd said no and asked him to leave. I'd kill him with my bare hands. Fucking bastard. He stood about four inches above my six foot-one-inch frame, but it didn't matter. I had the element of surprise, and I also felt as if I suddenly possessed the strength of fifty men. Before he knew what was happening, I had him against the wall with my hands around his throat.

"She said no, ass wipe," I said through clenched teeth. "And she asked you to leave. Want to try and fucking explain why you're still here?"

I didn't give him a chance to explain because no matter what he said, he'd only piss me off more. Keeping my hold on his neck, I led him to the door, and shoved him through it. Slamming it shut and engaging the locks for good measure.

Still facing the door, I took three deep breaths before turning toward Mia.

She'd moved and was now sitting on the couch, her face buried in her hands. She wasn't crying, not that I could tell, anyway. But her shoulders were shaking.

Seeing her like that, visibly upset and vulnerable, made me want to go after Benjamin and pound him into the ground. The one thing that kept me from doing just that was Mia needed me more than I needed to hit him.

I didn't want to touch her, not after that. I was too afraid doing so would do nothing but upset her. There was no way any touch from me would bring her any measure of comfort. Hell, I wasn't even certain if she felt safe with me being in the room with her, but I'd be damned if I'd leave her alone until I was one hundred ten percent convinced she was fine.

I took a tentative seat on the couch beside her, careful not to accidentally touch her. "Mia?" I asked in a whisper. "Are you okay?"

She slowly lifted her head. "No," she answered and though I saw fear in her eyes, I saw something else that made me believe her when she said, "No, I'm not okay. But I will be."

"I know that for a fact. Don't you doubt it for a second."

She dipped her head as if suddenly shy and I once more held back from touching her. I cleared my throat. "Will you tell me what happened tonight?"

She nodded, but it took a few seconds before she started. When she did, however, even though her voice was low, it was strong. They had met in the lobby as planned and Benjamin suggested they hang out at the bar before heading somewhere to eat.

Mia said she was a bit tired which wasn't a

surprise to her. Traveling always made her feel that way. They spent longer in the bar than she'd anticipated and she couldn't figure out why. Several times she'd hinted at going to get something to eat, but Benjamin was never ready. Either he wanted to watch a replay of whatever sport the bar had on or else he would shake his head.

It wasn't until nearly two hours had passed that she finally stood up and told him she was getting something to eat. She didn't care if he stayed or went.

"He came with me," she said. "I told him I wasn't going out anywhere because it was too late and I was too tired and hungry. He shrugged and said that was fine."

"How did he act at dinner?" I asked, trying to wrap my head around what exactly had happened.

"That's the strange thing, he wasn't anything like the way he was at the bar. He was much more in line with the guy I remembered him being. In a way, it felt like that time at the bar didn't happen or else it didn't happen like I remembered it."

"How much had you had to drink by this time?" I hated asking her, but I wanted to know if her judgment had somehow been compromised. I didn't place it past this guy not to drug her drink.

"That's the funny thing, I hadn't had anything.

In the bar I only had two tonic waters and I had iced tea for dinner." At my raised eyebrow, she continued. "I can't drink on an empty stomach."

"What happened after dinner?" I asked.

She hugged herself, rubbing her arms as she spoke. "Not much of anything. We lingered over our meal and by the time we left the restaurant, it was almost midnight. He asked if I'd like to go back to his room, but I said no."

"And he asked if he could walk you to yours?" I finished, guessing the rest.

She nodded. "I knew he'd try to get inside, but I never thought he'd use force." She closed her eyes. "Thank goodness you were awake and in the room next door. I can't imagine what would have happened if you hadn't shown up."

Unfortunately, I was almost positive she knew exactly what would have happened if I hadn't been able to get to her in time. That was probably the reason for the shiver that ran through her body.

"Are you cold?" I asked, standing and feeling the need to do something. "Can I get you a blanket or some water?"

"Do you know what I'd really like?"

"No, tell me." *Please.*

She looked up at me and glanced away quickly, biting her bottom lip.

"Mia?" I sat back down.

"Will you hold me?"

It took a few seconds for her request to make sense in my head. "Are you sure?" I asked.

"Yes." She shifted toward me, so close our legs touched. "I trust you and I feel safe with you."

There was no way I could turn her down. Not when she made that request and looked at me with those trusting eyes of hers. She could ask for the moon and I'd try to get it for her. The intensity I felt about her shocked me.

I put a hesitant arm around her, but she wanted nothing to do with my hesitation. She took my hand and pulled my arms tighter around her shoulders while at the same time, moving even closer to me and tucking her head under my chin. It was only once she had settled herself that her body sagged against mine and the warm breath of her sigh caressed my neck.

"I was so tired after dinner," she said. "But now I don't think I could go to sleep if you made me."

I lowered my head, just a touch, so I could smell her hair. The scent was citrusy and reminded me of sunshine. "Do you want to call the police and report what happened?" I asked, because it was a question that had to be asked.

"No," she answered.

"Let me rephrase. Do you think you should report what happened?"

"I've been thinking about that and I don't know. I mean, if you look at it, nothing really happened."

"Only because I stopped it," I reminded her. Not that she needed or wanted a reminder, I was sure.

"But that doesn't take away from the fact that nothing happened." Without waiting for a response, she continued, "I'm not even sure if the police could do anything anyway. It's not like he lives here."

"I hate the thought of that scumbag getting away. Knowing you aren't going to report him makes me want to beat him up, just for the hell of it," I said, though I hope I kept just how angry I was with the man somewhat hidden for fear I might scare her.

She snuggled deeper into my arms. "He won't get away with anything. I firmly believe that karma is real and that she's also a bitch."

"Does that mean if I see him in the hotel tomorrow, I can't hit him?" Because if that was her assumption, she needed to know I wouldn't be able to hold back.

"No way. If you see him tomorrow, feel free to knock him a good one."

I pulled back just a bit. Just enough so she could see my face. I thanked her for having the confidence in me to lay Benjamin out. However, I had a feeling deep in my gut that told me Benjamin would no longer be listed as a guest of the hotel. That made me all sorts of happy. "I'm glad you feel that way," I told her. "Because I believe in karma, too. Except my karma has fists."

She laughed and my heart melted. "That's the best kind of karma there is."

For a second she was back to her happy-go-lucky self and her smile was so beautiful, I couldn't stop myself from running my thumb over her lips. So soft, just as I'd imagined and the most sensuous shade of pink I'd ever seen. I wanted to discover how she tasted. She sucked in a breath and I could have kicked myself. What had I been thinking to touch her like that? I was such an idiot.

"I'm sorry." I dropped my arm from around her shoulders and tried to push away from her.

She placed her hand on my knee. "No."

CHAPTER TEN

MIA

*B*eside me, Tenor flinched.

"What's wrong?" I asked him.

"I shouldn't have touched you." He closed his eyes and wouldn't look at me, but at least he'd stopped trying to get away from me. I was thankful for that. In his arms, I felt safe and protected.

"Why?" I asked him. "Because Benjamin turned out to be an ass? That's not your fault."

His eyes were open and he was looking at me. That was better than him not looking at me, but something was still off. "I know it's not my fault, but you've had an emotional night and I shouldn't do anything to add to that."

It sounded very practical, but practical wasn't what I needed or wanted at the moment. "Maybe you're not adding to it," I said and shifted the tiniest bit toward him. If he'd noticed, he didn't say anything or try to scoot away. "Maybe you're what I need to help me get over my emotional night." My own admission shocked the hell out of me.

I'd heard of the expression 'deer in the head-lights' but until that moment, I'd never actually seen it on a person. Tenor looked exactly like that. It was almost funny. Was he scared of me?

But no, I realized. He'd kept my date from assaulting me and in thanks I acted as if I was going to jump his bones. Tenor was doing everything he could to be a perfect gentleman and I wasn't letting him fulfill the role.

The thing was, he was right. It had been a highly emotional night. I wasn't in the best place or frame of mind to be doing anything. But in that moment, sitting beside him, all that paled in comparison to the fact that I wanted him. I didn't want to want him, but my libido didn't seem to care.

And I was pretty certain he wanted me as well.

The realization was shocking and unexpected. At least to me. And the strange thing was, I didn't want to fight it.

But if we acted on those feelings tonight, we'd both regret it. Okay, I wouldn't regret it, but he would and I didn't want guilt of any kind to taint anything about us.

Then there was the fact that he was my boss. Fuck. Funny how I kept forgetting that at times. Plus, I didn't like him.

Right. I didn't believe it anymore either.

Either way I looked at it, if anything happened tonight, Tenor would feel guilty on both of those accounts. So my wants and needs would have to wait for another day when only the fact that he was my boss would be an issue. Tonight, however....

I tried to yawn and discovered it wasn't much of a stretch for me to let out a big one. Beside me, Tenor let out a deep breath, obviously overjoyed at my fatigue.

"Sleepy?" he asked.

I nodded. "But if you don't mind, can I ask a favor?"

"Of course," he replied, but he hesitated before saying it and he looked very tired himself. Hadn't he said before I left to see Benjamin that he was going to bed? And yet, here he was, still up and making sure I was okay after running a would-be attacker from my room.

"I'm sorry," I said. "You should be sleeping and because of me, you're still up."

"Don't even think about apologizing," he said and even though he still looked tired, there was a strength in his expression and his tone left no room for arguing. "I'm not sorry at all. I'm glad I'm awake because I can't think about what would have happened if I wasn't."

I couldn't look at him. It wasn't fair to him no matter what he said.

"Mia." He gently took my chin, turning it gently until I faced him. "I mean it. Don't even think about feeling guilty. Okay?"

His fingers were softer than I'd imagined they'd be. It was a bit odd in a way. There was no part of him that was soft. Perhaps, then, it was only his touch that was soft? I knew from watching him kick Benjamin out how hard he could be otherwise.

He smiled at me and I couldn't stop myself, I smiled back. "Okay." The words slipped from my lips without me even thinking about them. I wasn't one hundred percent sure what I was agreeing to.

Right. No guilt.

Oh well, it wouldn't be my first lie. Probably not my last either.

"Now," he said. "What was the favor you wanted to ask me?"

As much as I'd just admitted to myself that I had

lied and would do it again, there was no way I could do with him watching me the way he was. "Would you mind horribly much if I asked you to stay with me tonight?" I regretted it as soon as I spoke the question and saw the trepidation in his eyes, but whatever negative response I'd anticipated, never materialized.

His voice was calmer than I'd expected when he asked, "Here in your room? Or here in your bed?"

My bed. Though I only wanted his comfort, I was unable to keep more intimate images out of my mind. Images I thought would scare me after the last few hours, but didn't. "It really doesn't matter. It's only, I don't want to be alone."

"Do you think he'll come back?"

Shit. That thought hadn't entered my mind, but with his words, I could imagine it happening. He wouldn't, would he? I didn't think so, but what if I was wrong? What if he did? Suddenly, I was freezing. Or I guessed that was why I felt so cold.

"Fuck," Tenor said, turning toward me and putting his arms around me. He pulled me close, all the while whispering, "He's not coming anywhere near you. Not tonight. Not ever. He'll have to get through me first."

And once more, I was safe.

* * *

He ended up staying in my room all night. For about an hour we sat on the couch, but it eventually grew uncomfortable. Tenor stood and took my hand, ensuring I'd follow as he walked to his room to gather a few things before heading back to mine.

When we were once again locked safely inside, he shuffled me off into the bathroom to change into my pjs. I felt the urge to take a shower, even though I'd taken one before meeting Benjamin. Symbolically washing him away, I supposed. Freshly clean and comfortable in my soft cotton sleep shorts and tee, I crawled into bed. I was asleep before Tenor made it out of the bathroom.

I woke up sometime in the middle of the night to find his arms around me while he slept on top of the covers. I smiled and snuggled closer, wondering how in the world I ever thought he was an asshole.

Maybe it was that revelation in the early morning hours that made it so hard to believe I heard him correctly at breakfast.

"I have to be honest, Mia. As much as I'm attracted to you, you and I can never happen."

CHAPTER ELEVEN

TENOR

I wasn't sure why I lied to her during breakfast. I probably didn't sound very convincing, because Mia froze for a brief second before she continued eating. She took her time chewing and swallowing her bite of pancake.

"Okay."

That was all she said. *Okay.* My proclamation didn't seem to bother her a bit. I was shocked. I thought she'd push back or argue with me. Anything. But the calm, cool, and collected way she continued to eat her breakfast told me one of two things:

Either she wasn't attracted to me at all, which implied I'd read her all wrong or...

She thought I was completely filled with horse shit.

I was more inclined to go with the second option. I was, after all, a matchmaker and there was no way possible I could have been that wrong about the signals she was throwing my way the night before.

And if option two was correct, she didn't believe a word I'd just said. Not that I did either.

I cleared my throat. "Can we at least pretend that I meant what I said?"

She gave me a sultry grin. "You're the boss."

That shouldn't have made me hard. It really shouldn't have. But damn...

"Did you sleep okay last night?" I asked. Maybe a change of subject would help.

Help what? I didn't know.

"I did. And if I didn't say it before, thank you for everything you did."

"No need to thank me, Mia."

I wasn't sure she would thank me if she knew how much I'd enjoyed holding her during the night or how I'd spent a lot of the night battling my erection.

We fell into silence as we finished eating our breakfast. We would start meetings soon and we had plans to continue business through lunch. But tonight *I* had plans.

Plans that didn't involve Benjamin. Meetings. Or

anything remotely similar to behavior my lawyer would approve of.

Which made me wonder why I even spoke that lie about us never happening. Maybe I should have worded it differently. Much differently.

BY THE TIME we made it back to the hotel at four that afternoon, I was tired of meetings. They had gone extremely well and if things continued on the path I envisioned, Bachelor International could be a franchise by the end of the year. That made the business part of myself very happy. Now if I could get things worked out with Mia, life would be sweet indeed.

She had been impressive during the meetings, exactly the way I'd thought she'd be. She was whip smart and asked a few questions I hadn't thought of. In fact, seeing her today and the easy way she fit in by my side, like she'd always been there, had me thinking, it might be in the company's best interest for her to be in charge of the Atlanta office, once it was up and running.

The only downside being she'd have to move to Atlanta, and I didn't want to go there right now.

Our cab pulled up to the hotel. I glanced to the woman at my side. Unlike me, Mia seemed to be energized by the meetings. Her cheeks were flushed and I swore if I touched her, I'd feel an undercurrent of electricity pulse through her.

Had she not bounced out of the cab the second it pulled to a stop, I would have been able to test that theory when I helped her out. As it was, I felt fortunate she didn't take off and disappear into the hotel before I finished paying our driver.

"Would you like to have dinner with me tonight?" I asked her before she could sprint away from me.

Her eyes automatically went to the restaurant in the lobby. Like I'd take her there. "At the risk of sounding conceited—"

"Too late," she said, but at least she smiled when she said it. "If you have to say 'at the risk of,' you know you are what you're saying you're not." Her forehead wrinkled. "I'm not sure that came out right."

I didn't want to try to unravel that sentence. "I made us reservations at a well-known, but out of the way place near the Chattahoochee River. It came highly recommended."

Her eyebrows raised in interest, but she wasn't

about to give in that easily. "Highly recommended by who?"

Busted.

"By the hotel concierge when I asked for a nice place to eat." I didn't add the second part of my request to the concierge. That I also wanted a place that was quiet and on the romantic side. Fortunately for me, the young woman working the desk when I made my request knew exactly what I was going for. She said she knew just the place and in fact, had been there a few weekends ago for a wedding.

"Pretty sure of yourself, Tenor Butler. Aren't you?" She teased.

"I was until right this second."

She laughed and I grinned at how much I loved that sound. "I love how you never back down from telling the truth."

I never backed down from telling the *partial* truth, but I wasn't about to admit to that at the moment. Not when I'd almost gotten her to agree to dinner. "Is that a yes?"

She wasn't ready to give into me just yet. "What time did you make them for?"

"Six," replied. "Plenty of time for you to shower, change, and for us to get there. And if we're early, we can walk by the river."

Her eyes lit up. "We can?"

"Yes, and if we get there and we don't have time to walk before dinner, there's plenty of time after." I wanted to walk either before or after dinner so we could get to know each other better. The fact she wanted to do so as well, made me want to take her in my arms and kiss her.

"Yes. Let's do it."

By that time, we'd made it to our rooms. "I'll knock on your door in an hour."

"I'll be ready."

I could only hope I was, because I had a feeling tonight would change everything.

CHAPTER TWELVE

MIA

I'll admit I was a bit on the leery side when Tenor asked me to dinner. For a second, I feared he might be asking me out of pity or obligation. But when he'd said he'd gotten a recommendation from the hotel, I knew it was neither of those two. He'd asked me because he wanted to.

Who could turn Tenor Butler down? Especially when he got that smile on his face. Not the plastic smile he'd had before his first cup of coffee. Not the fake smile he'd worn until about ten-thirty this morning. Not even the businessman smile he'd donned during our massive number of meetings. None of those.

No, I was talking about the panty-dropping, *I can picture you naked and want to do dirty and nasty and Earth-shaking things to your body that will take all night and half of tomorrow* smile.

Yes. Fuck yes. Take me now, hard against the wall yes.

Lucky for me, I made it safely into my room before I could voice my thoughts out loud. Though I'll admit, I just barely made it. I was desperately aroused when the door closed behind me. Hearing him roughly command, "Lock it, Mia. And I mean it," didn't help any at all.

My heart was pounding. I was breathing heavily and I had never felt so empty in my entire life. It wouldn't take much for me to sail right over the edge. I gave serious thought to taking care of the issue with my own hands or hell, even humping the couch, but in the end I decided not to.

Being aroused, I told myself, would give dinner an edge. Make the entire experience sharper. And when I did finally get some relief, it'd be incredible.

Yeah, I actually convinced myself of that.

Come to find out, that wasn't only a bad mistake, it was a ridiculously stupid bad mistake. Take it from me, the only thing at dinner that needs an edge is your knife. The only thing that needs to be sharp is your wit. And maybe his.

But I was totally and completely correct about how incredible my release would be.

WE DIDN'T HAVE time to walk by the river before we ate. I'd thought when he'd first brought it up that it'd be highly unlikely we would. Thanks to the Atlanta traffic, as soon as we arrived and checked in, we were told our table was ready.

It didn't help that I was a little bit late getting ready. Don't ask me why, but it took forever for me to decide what to wear. Ridiculous, right? I mean, it wasn't even like I had that much to pick from. I was on a business trip with a suitcase to select from. It wasn't like I was at home and had an entire closet.

Tenor didn't say a word when he knocked on my door so we could grab a cab for dinner. I met him in a hotel robe and suggested he wait on the couch for me. He waited in silence, looking far too good in his custom-made suit. No, it was only when I stepped into the room and stood before him, that he broke his silence.

"You look fantastic," he said with a grin. He stood and held out his arm for me.

I couldn't help but to compare his actions and

behavior to that of Benjamin's the night before. Granted, with Benjamin, even though things had been off with him from the start, it wasn't until the very end that it had gone really, really bad.

There was nothing off about Tenor. Nothing at all even gave the hint of being off. As my mind began to process that, any remaining tension left. I knew Tenor would never do anything like Benjamin, no matter what we had been doing. Taking a deep breath, I let the tension out of my back and shoulders, relaxing for what felt like the first time months. The stress and emotional turmoil over mama and the business melted away.

Once in the cab, we made small talk as we travelled to the restaurant. I found it hard to keep my eyes off Tenor. The blue shirt he had on somehow made his eyes seem darker than normal and honestly, every part of him moved with an unmistakable grace that drew me to him.

"I guess we can take a walk after dinner," Tenor said after we sat down. "I didn't expect traffic to be that bad." He chuckled at my raised eyebrow. "Yeah, I don't know what I was thinking either."

"Probably better that we walk after dinner anyway," I said looking over the menu. "From the looks of this menu, we'll need to burn off some calories." Everything on the menu sounded delicious. Not to mention how delicious it looked after a quick glance around the tables near us. "I'm tempted to order one of everything. The only thing stopping me is those portions I'm seeing aren't exactly small. There's no way I could eat all that food and it'd be a sin to throw it out."

"Don't tempt me, I just might go ahead and order it all. But you're right, it wouldn't be good to waste it. I think I'll go with the pork tenderloin, instead." He closed his menu. "What are you thinking?"

"Trying to decide which fish to go with and leaning toward the cod with crawfish."

The waiter came by shortly thereafter and recommended the cod, so I went with that. After he walked away, I leaned back in my chair.

"Are you happy with the way everything went today?" I asked. I'd been surprised at how much I'd enjoyed both the meetings and working alongside Tenor. We made a good pair.

He nodded. "I've been wanting to expand for a long time and I think the Atlanta location would be a logical next step. I've also been thinking about bringing on a partner."

"Will you stay in Boston or will you move down here?" I was almost afraid to ask, but I feared not knowing more than I was afraid of asking. Maybe if he hired a partner, that person could move to Atlanta.

"I might come down here every once in a while, but I have no desire to move from Boston. I'll hire someone to run the place here." He shot me a playful look. "You wouldn't be interested in moving to Atlanta would you?"

That wasn't why he'd asked me to come with him on this trip, was it? Surely he didn't think I'd be interested in moving, did he? A chill washed over me. What if it was?

"It was a joke, Mia," he said with a grin. "And not a very good one, either based on how pale you just got."

I sucked air into my lungs. "You don't want me to move to Atlanta?"

"No, and I'm sorry. I won't joke like that again."

I had no reason to doubt him. He'd never lied to me before and I saw no reason why he'd start now. But suddenly I wondered what had been his plan in bringing me on board at Bachelor International. Was there a specific reason or had he only been thinking to eliminate his competition? "Was there another reason you hired me that I don't know about?" I managed to ask.

"I know how you feel about our questionnaires," he said. "You've made no secret of your dislike of our multiple choice questions."

He was certainly right about that. I bobbed my head in a slight nod.

"While I would like to do away with that questionnaire and completely redo it, it does have a winning track record and I know my staff would not look kindly on changing to something that in their opinion is unproven."

I almost stopped him to remind him that it was not totally unproven, but he'd known of my success with it.

"What I would like for you to do, is to try it out with our international division and see how it works. Run some analysis and compare the two methods. If you find it's significantly better, I'll have the data I need to implement it company-wide."

He still wanted me on the international team? I'd picked up early in my time at work that the international part of Bachelor International was different to Tenor and that he held that part of his business separate from the other part. He'd mentioned it when we'd first discussed my role in his company, but up until our trip here, I'd been busy just going over the day-to-day of Bachelor International.

"You look as though that surprises you," he said.

"I know how important the international division is to you."

He lifted his wine glass and took a sip. I had to force myself not to stare at his lips. I wondered how they would feel on mine with the slightest hint of wine on them. I was certainly no longer chilly. "It's very important to me," he said. "And now you know how important I think you are to the success of my business."

It warmed me inside to know he valued what I brought to his company and he trusted me with such an important division.

Our entrees arrived at that moment and after we took a bite, neither of us were able to focus on anything other than how delicious our food was. By the time we'd stopped gushing about it, he asked me about baseball and we bonded over our love of the Red Sox.

The sun had just disappeared for the day when we stepped outside. I thought I'd be chilly with the sun down, but it seemed as if I'd underestimated how hot it could still be in the South after dark.

"It's so peaceful out here," I said as Tenor led the way to a well-traveled path along the river.

"Hard to believe we're close to the city, isn't it?" He had turned ever so slightly to the left and positioned as he was, I had an incredible view of his profile. Everything about him called to me and I'd never wanted a man so much. And of course, because the universe enjoyed screwing with me, he had to be my boss and therefore, completely unattainable.

"Lately it seems everything about my life is hard to believe," I said.

He turned in surprise, concern marring his features. "What do you mean?"

"I don't mean it in a bad way," I hastened to tell him. "Not at all. It's just.... If you had told me three months ago, I'd be here with you?" I shook my head. "I'd have laughed in your face."

Even as little as one month ago, I'd thought us to be too different. And though in some ways we were, like our approach to matchmaking and our upbringings, we still seemed to complement the other.

I thought my statement would lighten the mood, but he came to a halt and turned to face me, all serious. "What part of this? The part that you're working for me or the part that we just had dinner?"

"Any of it," I whispered, the concern in his eyes nearly gutting me. "I wouldn't have believed any of it."

He was silent and wrinkled his forehead in thought. The wind blew an errant strand of hair in my eyes and before I could brush it out of the way, he beat me to it. His fingers felt better than I had imagined and my eyes slid shut at how gentle he could be.

"You're nothing like I thought you would be," I whispered.

He didn't move away, only shifted his hand so his thumb dropped to my lips and traced their outline. "How did you think I'd be?" he asked and the low sound combined with his touch made me warm and tingly inside.

"Conceited." I tilted my head. "Kind of like a mix between a used car salesman and a scuzzy lawyer." He lifted an eyebrow. "You asked."

"I did, didn't I? I suppose no one has ever accused you of not holding back, have they?"

"I've never seen the point in lying about how I feel." I wanted him closer, but I hesitated to move, afraid he'd back away.

"What do you think of me now?" he whispered and leaned in a bit.

"That you're a dangerous man."

In truth, we had stopped at a secluded part of the river path. He pushed his thumb against the seam of my mouth and without thinking, I sucked his finger inside. The hiss he gave in response morphed into a moan and I sucked harder.

"You have it all wrong," he said and his voice was rough. "You're the dangerous one."

I let his thumb fall from my lips. "Me?"

"Yes." He took a step closer and in doing so I felt his hardness. "You have me thinking things I should not think about an employee."

"Funny you should say that. I was thinking you were making me feel things I know better than to feel about my boss."

And there it was, the knowledge and the wanting that was driving us both to distraction. But there was nothing we could do about it.

"What if..." he started but shook his head. "Nah, forget it."

"What?"

"I can't. Or closer to the truth, I shouldn't."

"Tell me." If he had figured out a way for us to happen, I wanted to know what it was. "Please."

"I thought we could pretend like when we're here, in Atlanta, that we're just Tenor and Mia. Not employee and employer. But I can't ask you to do that. It really doesn't change anything."

"I like it." While we weren't in Boston, we could pretend to be any ordinary couple.

"My attorney would disagree."

"Your attorney isn't here. I am. And I want you." I bumped my hip against him. I wasn't sure where this aggressive side of me had come from. It wasn't like me at all.

Tenor seemed to enjoy my new side. No sooner had I finished my sentence than he roughly took me in his arms. "I can't find it in me to keep coming up with reasons why we shouldn't do this."

"Good."

And still he hesitated. Damn it all.

"Would it help if I signed something saying anything we do I give my consent and will never seek to file a complaint?" I asked.

"Doubtful," he said. "A good lawyer would only have to say you signed under duress."

He wasn't going to take us any further. *Damn it all.*

"What's my name?" I asked, deciding to try something different.

"Mia."

"And what's your name?"

"Seriously?"

"Humor me."

"Tenor."

"Come here often, Tenor?" And then for good measure I batted my eyelashes.

It worked. He laughed.

Apparently, it was what he needed, a good laugh and a ridiculous role play, to break the *I'm your boss and we can't do this* mindset he'd been in for way too long. After a few seconds, he wasn't laughing anymore. His expression grew serious and his eyes darkened.

"God, Mia," he whispered. "What you do to me, I'll never be able to explain."

I ran my hands up his arms, delighting in the muscles under my fingertips. "You don't have to. I feel the same thing."

He lowered his head and I held my breath. I could practically feel his kiss and I was desperate to taste him. But right before his lips finally, *finally* brushed mine, a child's laughter broke through the quiet bliss of our wonderland, followed by an equally loud, "You'll never find me."

We managed to jump apart and to appear as nothing more than a couple out strolling and enjoying the beautiful setting when a pair of elementary school-aged boys ran up behind us.

"Strangers! Strangers!" One of them yelled. "Daddy!"

Tenor looked and me with a raised eyebrow. I shook my head. I didn't understand either. Surely they didn't think they would be the only ones out walking.

Within seconds, a couple, the parents I assumed by the way the two boys clung to them, appeared. The dad saw us and shot us both an apologetic look. "Sorry about that."

"No worries," Tenor said.

The mother took the boys off to the side of the path and I overheard snippets. "That's why I told you...." And, "Can't go off..."

Tenor and I left the family and headed back in the direction of the restaurant. We'd only gone a few steps when he said, "I know we needed to stop and go back to the hotel, but damn, isn't it a school night?"

I couldn't help but chuckle even though my libido didn't find anything humorous about the situation. "Who knew you didn't have to have kids in order to be cock-blocked by them?"

"Cock-blocked by a stranger's kids on a school night."

We both laughed and since by then we were within earshot of the restaurant, our laughter drew the attention of the few people hanging outside. Tenor cleared his throat and asked the attendant outside to call a cab for us.

As we waited for our ride, he draped an arm around my shoulders. The heat of his touch reminded my body of what we'd been doing before we were interrupted and hopefully what we'd be doing once we made it back to our room.

I nearly groaned as I remembered the long-ass drive from the hotel to our current location.

"That didn't sound like a happy sound," Tenor teased and I realized I hadn't held it inside as well as I thought I had.

"Who's idea was it again to make dinner reservations so far away from our hotel?" I asked as I squeezed my thighs together in a useless attempt to alleviate my need.

CHAPTER THIRTEEN

That would have been me. Mia shot me a teasing glance as she hopped into the back of our cab. At the time, it seemed like a great idea. The restaurant was highly rated, it had a beautiful setting, and I'd suspected if I got Mia away from the city, we could turn our attention to the ever growing attraction between us and to finally do something about it.

I'll even admit I thought about stealing kisses along the pathway as we strolled near the river. What I had not ever once thought about was having the kiss interrupted before it could even happen.

Damn it. I'd been so fucking close to finding out just how Mia tasted, what her lips felt like under mine, and how her body would react when it came into contact with mine. She was a much better poker player than I was. I knew she had to be a little upset at the untimely appearance of the young family, but she held it together much better than I did. Or at least better than how I thought I did.

I glanced to my side. Traffic going back to the hotel wasn't nearly as bad as it had been on our way out. However, it was still a busy city and it was taking longer than I wanted for us to make it back. Once we were there, alone...

Mia sat to my left, looking out her window. If I looked, I'd probably be able to meet her eyes in the glass, but I didn't want to just yet. Her hand rested in the space between us and I let myself inch my fingers forward until her hand was completely under mine. I wiggled my fingers in between hers until they were interlocked and then I caressed her palm, right at the base of her thumb, making slow and sensual passes.

The slight hitch in her breathing was the only sign she gave that she was even aware I was in the cab. I smiled. Frankly, that wasn't enough for me. I needed to know she wanted to explore this *thing* between us as badly and as thoroughly as I did. I wanted to know that I made her heart race and that she wouldn't be able to rest or sleep soundly again until we'd given into it at least once.

Not that I was under any misguided allusion that having her once would be enough. I knew it wouldn't be. Just as I knew we could both vow that once we returned to Boston we could pretend we left it all back in Atlanta, but that didn't mean we wouldn't remember. That we would forget the other person's touch. It drove me mad that even with that foresight, I still wanted her with an ache that defied logic and damn it all, I wanted to know she wanted me, too. That she burned for me as intently as I burned for her.

I moved my hand away from hers and placed it on her knee. Her head jerked away from the window and she turned to look at me.

"What?" I smiled.

"What are you doing?" she asked with a sultry smile. "Trying to be sneaky?"

"I love this dress on you." As I talked, I moved my hand up her leg, slipping my fingers under the material, careful not to snag the delicate hose she wore. "I know I told you that earlier this evening, but something has my head in a quandary."

"What is that?" She glanced at the cab driver and then back to me. I could have told her she didn't need to worry about the driver hearing us. He was completely focused on traffic at the moment and mumbling under his breath in a language I didn't recognize, at the drivers sharing the road with us.

"I don't remember seeing any panty lines." I'd reached her inner thighs and I stopped my fingers there for a moment, stroking her. She felt so good and it was killing me not to move my hand higher. "Are you not wearing panties?"

Her cheeks flushed, so I knew she heard me even though she turned her head back to look out the window. I almost laughed. Like I'd give up that easily.

I let my fingers inch a little higher along her inner thigh. "If you don't answer," I whispered. "I'll be forced to check it out myself. And I have to say, I don't mind putting in the time to research the issue thoroughly."

"You wouldn't dare," she said, still looking out her window.

"Are you sure about that? Because I'm pretty sure I would." I let my fingers drift up her thigh to show her how serious I was. I think she got it, because she trembled under my touch. "Try me."

I had to give her credit. She kept her face turned to the window the entire time we talked, though every so often, she'd glance at our driver. But he never paid us the slightest bit of attention.

"No," she whispered so softly, I almost couldn't hear her. "I'm not wearing any."

I had thought I was fairly aroused before she admitted to being completely bare under her dress. But my cock jerked to full attention and pressed painful against its confines when she whispered she wasn't wearing panties.

I balled the fist that wasn't on her thigh and took a deep breath. "I think I need to verify."

But she moved faster than I'd anticipated, drawing her skirt down and crossing her legs. For all intents and purposes, shutting me out of the Promised Land for now. "No." She took my hand from her thigh and placed it back on the seat between us. "Not here. You can verify, but we have to wait until we're in our rooms."

"Or in the elevator if no one is there with us." We might as well be on the two thousandth floor for as long as it would take us to make it up to our rooms.

"In our rooms," she repeated. "You know the elevators have cameras. I'm not going to be the security guards' entertainment tonight. Nor do I want the video of me naked from the waist down in an elevator to make it on the company's secret holiday video they pass out this year."

"What the hell? What secret video?" I asked,

trying to make heads or tails out of what she was saying.

"You didn't see that news documentary?" she asked and then continued when I shook my head. "Some of the security companies, you know the ones that work out of high rises or hotels and apartments? They're all the time seeing people do crazy shit in elevators. They save the best clips in one file and then at their holiday parties, they play them all."

"Really?" I asked, even though it made total sense to me. After all, if I were working security at a high rise and shit got boring, I could easily see myself looking through security feeds for some entertainment. "On second thought, I get it."

"You do?"

"The companies aren't doing anything wrong or illegal by having cameras and like you said, everyone knows they're there. So really, if you want to get frisky in an elevator, it's pretty much on par with public sex. Odds are you'll be seen by someone. Of course, that doesn't mean it's okay for these places to keep the video and use it for their own enjoyment. If that's not illegal, it should be. At the least, it's unethical."

"I agree with you there," she said, an unmasked

look of victory in her eyes. "And look. There's our hotel."

"Damn, you're good," I said once it hit me that she'd kept me occupied and thinking about something other than how naked she was under her dress. "I didn't even pick up on what you were doing until you pointed out the hotel."

By then, the cab had stopped in front of the lobby. I paid the driver who smiled and thanked me, and then I turned back to offer Mia my hand. We walked silently to the elevators. Once we were inside, alone except for the ever watchful security camera and staff, I leaned over and whispered, "Part of me wants to bust out into 'We wish you a Merry Christmas'. Matter of fact, if I didn't suck so bad at singing, I think I would. But I won't because the one thing worse than me naked on film is me singing on film."

"No way, the worst would be you naked *and* singing on film."

I gave her shoulder a playful shove. "Hey, you've never even heard my singing."

"To hear the way you talk about it, I should consider that a blessing. But I can't believe you're that bad of a singer. Seriously, I've never seen you fail at anything."

We were almost to our floor and I ached with the need to touch her, to do something about the awareness that hummed between us. "Just hang around me long enough and you will. I'm not perfect, nor do I claim to be."

In the seconds before the doors opened, she shifted so she stood between me and the door. "Thank goodness for that. I have no desire to be with a perfect person. I think that would suck. Especially in bed."

I tried to take my time getting to our rooms so Mia wouldn't catch on to how badly I wanted her. Halfway to the doors, I realized she was probably already aware of just how much I wanted her. Hell, my cock had been pressed against her when we were by the river. Why try to hide it now? "I'm ready to show you just how not perfect I can be," I told her. "Your room or mine?"

She lifted a finger to her lips and tilted her head in an exaggerated thinking act. "Hmmm..."

I chuckled and dragged her into mine, simply because it was open and I was tired of waiting. I half expected her to play fight or resist, but she didn't, which told me she was tired of waiting, too. Thank fuck.

I came to a stop right beside the bed. Before we

went any further, I felt it necessary to reiterate the important points. "If you don't want this, we don't have to do anything." I tried not to think about how I was getting ready to utterly and completely potentially fuck up everything. My job. My company. My name. My reputation. Everything. "I mean, we could just say goodnight and fly home tomorrow. There's nothing stopping you from turning around and walking out that door."

She looped her arms around my neck. "Tenor?"

I swallowed. "Yes?"

"Shut up."

I didn't have a chance to let it sink in that she was staying. Why had I thought she'd leave? There was no time to ask, because before I could form the words, her lips were on mine and the only thing running through my mind was the word FINALLY.

Her lips were soft and sweet, and they parted beneath mine, allowing me to taste her fully. I needed more. More of her. More of her mouth. More of her body pressed against mine. My fingers fumbled with the zipper on the back of the dress. I couldn't get it unzipped and I felt like a fifteen-year-old virgin. I'd never had trouble undressing anyone.

I pulled away. "I can't get this dress off of you, so I either need you to turn around so I can get it or else

I'll just pull it up and I can fuck you with it on." It was coarse and it was crass, but damn it all, it was what I felt and at that moment I needed inside her too badly to be waylaid for even a second by an unco-operative dress.

"I can't mess this dress up. It's not mine." She wiggled out of my embrace and tuned so her back was to me, lifting her hair up and out of the way. "Can you help me get it off? I need to hang it up."

Normally, I'd ask what the hell was so important about the dress, but in this case, the sooner the dress was off her and safely on a hanger meant the sooner I'd get to have my hands, fingers, and lips all over her gorgeous naked body.

I took a moment to simply enjoy the way she looked before me with her back facing me, her hair pulled back in a way that exposed her nape. I stepped close and breathed in the scent of her. Citrus and sunshine. I'd never look at an orange the same.

I took the zipper tab and slowly pulled it down, revealing the smooth skin of her back inch by tortuous inch. I reached her waist and held myself back from pressing my lips to her spine.

"There you go," I said, surprised by the rough-ness of my own voice. "If you don't want that dress ripped off you, I suggest you get it on a hanger quickly."

She sucked in a surprised breath and I couldn't help but grin.

"That's right, Mia. My restraint is wearing thin. I'm about five seconds away from ravishing that hot body of yours. Better hurry."

She moved quickly, stepping out of and hanging the dress up in a matter of seconds. My eyes followed her nearly naked body as she walked back to me wearing only an ice blue lace bra and a garter belt with hose. Totally unexpected since she told me she wasn't wearing panties and it was hot as hell. I may have growled.

"Damn, Mia," I said. "I don't think I've ever known anyone who wore garters."

She turned to the left, just enough so I could see how they framed her perfect ass. "You like?"

Instead of giving her a yes or no, like she expected, I unzipped my pants and shoved them down my hips along with my boxer briefs. Her eyes grew large as she took in my erection. "Does that answer your question?"

"I'm not sure, why don't you bring it over here so I can have a better look," she said in a sex kitten voice that made me harder.

I took a step forward and if the way she was looking at my cock wasn't bad enough, as I move closer, the tip of her tongue peeked out between her lips. Fucking. Hell. I was going to explode before I ever touched her. I stopped a few feet in front of her, thinking maybe I could hold out until I was inside her.

"I don't know," she said. "I need to get even closer." She lifted her head and met my gaze. Then, with a smile filled with sensual mischief, she lowered herself to her knees. I put my hands on her head to stop her, but she must have taken my reaction as encouragement because she proceeded to take as much of my length as possible into her mouth.

Fuck. The feel of her all warm and wet around me.

It took all my strength not to hold her head steady and thrust my whole cock into her mouth, to open her throat and fuck her face as hard as I could. "Careful," I warned. "I'm dangerously close to the edge and would rather be inside your pussy when I get there."

With a sigh, she fell back to her heels. "Maybe later then?"

I wasn't sixteen anymore, so I wasn't sure if it would be possible if she meant later tonight. Then again, as aroused as I'd been whenever I was with her lately, it was altogether possible that it might not be out of the question.

"Later is a very long time," I said and pulled her up. I ran a finger along the edge of her garter belt where it hooked onto her hose. "This is so hot. I think I want you to keep it on."

Her cheeks flushed, but she didn't protest. I leaned down for another kiss, taking my time and letting my hands wander across her body. I cupped her ass and pulled her close, the lace scratchy against the small amount of skin on my chest not covered by my shirt.

I pulled back and tugged on her bra strap. "Oh, no. This won't do. Not at all."

She lifted an eyebrow. "Your shirt's still on."

"It'll have to wait." I pushed the straps from her shoulders. "Take it off."

Once upon a time, I'd do it myself. I had long since mastered the art of unhooking bras without looking at them. But somehow in the last few years it seemed the damn things had gotten more and more complicated. Spend twenty minutes trying to untangle an undergarment that was so complicated to put on and take off you needed an instruction manual and see how quickly your libido died.

"You're so bossy," she said, with a mocking eye roll, but did it anyway.

She dropped the bra to the floor and I walked us both backward until she was against the bed. I pushed on her shoulders gently until she sat down.

"Come to the edge and spread your legs for me, beautiful," I said, going to my knees. "Let me see you."

Some women were overly shy when I wanted to get my mouth on them. Mia wasn't like that and it turned me on more to know she was so confident in her own skin and the way she owned her sexuality.

"Lay back if you want to," I told her. "Because I'm going to take my time tasting you and you have to come at least once before you get my cock again."

She didn't say anything, but got into the position I wanted her and stayed there while I did exactly what I said I would. I tasted and explored her until her knees shook and her fists clutched the sheets at her side. Only when she started making little panting sounds, did I start licking her clit.

It only took three strokes of my tongue until she clenched around me in release. Even then, I didn't pull back, but slipped two fingers deep inside her and kept up with the gentle, but relentless, sweeps of my tongue along her sensitive spot.

"Tenor," she groaned, pulling at my shoulders. "Please."

I lifted my head long enough to say, "Please what? You taste so good, I might do this all night."

She let out a string of garbled words. I couldn't be exactly sure, but I was almost positive she was cussing me out in another language.

"If you ask for what you want," I spoke while intermittently nibbling her skin. "You might get it."

Nothing but more garbled words. I moved us higher on the bed and suckled one of her nipples.

"Oh, God. Tenor."

I smiled against her skin, kissed her other nipple. "What do you want, beautiful?" I asked before drawing it deep inside my mouth.

"Fuck me." She grasped my shirt. "And get this off."

"You take it off."

She sat up and with a fierce determination began to unbutton my shirt. She did fairly well until about the fourth button. She mumbled something before finally taking the fabric in her hands. With a grunt and a hard pull, she ripped the rest of the buttons off. It might have been the hottest thing I'd ever seen and though I thought it damn near impossible, I grew harder.

"You just ruined my shirt," I said in mock outrage, tugging it off.

She shrugged. "Then you should have taken it off the first time I asked you."

I couldn't argue with that so I gave her a kiss instead. She parted her lips and I moved my tongue inside in a slow and sensual way that mimicked how I planned to take her. At first. My fingers brushed down her arms, across her belly, and went even lower, stroking between her legs to ensure she was still wet. She was. I moaned into her mouth, pleased with the knowledge of how I turned her on.

I slid my fingers out and she gave a tiny cry in protest. "I'm going to fill you up with something better," I promised. "Just let me get the condom on." I had a few waiting on the nightstand. I grabbed one and rolled it up my dick, all the while she watched me. The hunger in her eyes turned me on. "How should I give it to you the first time?" I asked, giving myself a hard stroke because her eyes grew wide each time I did. "Do you want me to fuck you hard or would you prefer slow?" I wasn't sure I could be slow, but if that was what she wanted, I'd give it a try.

She rose to her knees and pulled me to her. Her eyes were dark with lust and her voice husky. "I want you to fuck me as hard as you can with that massive cock of yours. I want it hard. I want it rough. And I want it dirty as hell."

Fuck, I loved this woman. "Then I've got you covered." I dipped my fingers inside her one more time.

Her grip on my arms tightened. "Honest to hell, Tenor, I promise you won't break me with your dick."

Since she seemed to be so flippant about the whole thing, I pushed her down on the bed and came up over her. "Spread your legs nice and wide for me so I can get my cock as deep as possible inside you." I felt her shift under me. "That's right. Just like that."

I lined myself up with her and watched her expression as I slowly entered her. Or at least, that had been my plan. In reality, she felt so good, my eyes nearly rolled to the back of my head in pleasure.

"Fuck, Mia," I groaned out her name, pulled out a little and thrust into her again.

"Again." She wrapped her legs around my waist and lifted her hips in invitation. "Harder."

I loved a vocal woman in bed. One who had no trouble telling me what turned her on the most and what she liked. Self-knowledge and self-confidence were sexy and hot. From the way I saw it, Mia had both. In spades.

I angled my hips to give her what she wanted and the resulting half gasp/half moan assured me I had. I took her hand and placed it on her clit. "Show me how you like to be touched."

Again, she showed no hesitation or shyness, but took my hand and together we stroked her where and how she enjoyed it the most. I knew she was getting close by the soft pants she made as I moved in and out of her and the way she trembled though her muscles were taunt with the strain to remain still.

"Let me see you come, Mia." I kept one hand on her clit, not giving her any way to hold back the release I knew was fast approaching.

With a strangled cry that might have been my name, she came and I was done for. "Mia," I managed to whisper. "You are stunning when you come." I feared she might think I said that to every woman I fucked, but the truth was, I'd never said it before.

She smiled and looked blissful and sated. Or at least she did until I rocked my hips and then she let out a groan as I moved in and out of her a few times. "You haven't come yet," she said, like she was telling me something I didn't know.

"Ladies first." I wasn't holding still, but I had slowed my pace down. Mia's eyelids fluttered as I pressed deep inside her. "I want you to come again for me."

She giggled. "If you insist."

"I do." I slid out of her and stroked myself. "Get on your hands and knees. I want to take you from behind. You'll be even tighter."

Her eyes grew hazy with lust and she hurried to get in position. I kept one hand on my cock and stroked her backside with the other. "You have a gorgeous ass." She giggled again and added an ass wiggle as well. I thoroughly enjoyed how playful she was in the bedroom. Joining in, I let out a chuckle while giving her backside a satisfying snack.

That only made her giggle more, but the giggles died when I placed my cock back at her entrance.

"Tenor," she moaned.

"You going to come for me again?"

She nodded and I slid partially inside her, both of us enjoying the slow way I filled her. "You feel so fucking good, Mia."

And she did. Better than I'd imagined she would be. Better than I'd ever experienced. And better than anything I knew I'd ever experience again.

Normally, withholding my own release wasn't an issue. I'd never had any problems ensuring my part-ners experienced many orgasms. I'd always been confident in my abilities as a lover. Never had I second guessed decisions, wondering if she would like what I had planned or if I was pleasing her, but I couldn't get that voice inside my head to stop questioning if she was enjoying herself.

Each time I touched her I fell deeper and deeper into her spell. Every thrust into her body was a way to bring me closer to her, a useless attempt to try and bind myself with her. I could make all the jokes in the world and say I was just horny or Mia was hot. But the truth hit me as I took her from behind.

I wanted more than the pleasure of her body. I wanted to breathe her in until she became a part of my very soul. And for one of the few times in my life, I was scared to let someone in that deep.

I clung to her as my release swept over me.

CHAPTER FOURTEEN

*I*t was almost as if I'd been transported to an alternate universe. I still couldn't believe it. I was in Tenor Butler's bed. Tenor. Butler. Not only that, but we'd just had what had to be the absolute best sex in the entire world. Or at least the best I'd ever had. I shivered remembering how rough his voice was as he moved inside me. How he'd grabbed and held onto me when he came.

His arms tightened around me. "Are you cold?"

I turned in his embrace, relishing the feel of our bodies being wrapped together the way they were and hummed. "Not it the slightest. I was remembering."

He kissed the top of my head. "Good things?"

"Oh, yes." I didn't add anything else, because,

honestly, he seemed a little distracted. I didn't feel comfortable trying to dig deeper, though. It wasn't like we were best friends or anything.

I didn't actually know what we were. Other than a couple who had probably gone further than they should have. Fuck. What had we done?

Though I really didn't want to think about the ramifications of what we'd just done, there didn't seem to be a way around it. It was pretty hard to ignore, given that we were both naked and in his bed.

Suddenly, the blissful *damn, that was good* feeling I had was replaced with an uncomfortable, *damn, that was a bad idea*. But like my mom had often told me, "You can't pour the milk back into the carton after it spills." It wasn't that I'd never understood what she meant when she said it, but I didn't understand exactly how impossible it was to pour the spilled milk back into the carton until that very second.

In reality, I felt a little sick to my stomach. I was now *that* girl. The one who slept with the boss. The one everyone whispered about behind her back. Would the entire office pick up on the fact that we'd slept together? Tenor had said he'd never done anything like this before, but should I simply take his word on that? Would he really admit it if it was something he did all the time? Doubtful.

I didn't realize I was restlessly moving until Tenor asked, "Are you okay? Do you need to use the bathroom?"

I didn't, but that gave me the excuse I needed to leave his bed. "Yes, sorry. I'll just be a minute."

He let go of me and I hurried across the floor to the bathroom. Once inside, I turned the light on, squinting at its brightness. After a few seconds, I slowly opened my eyes, only to wish I hadn't as soon as I did. Surely to goodness that wasn't me in the mirror. That wide-eyed woman with the just-kissed, swollen lips and the *I've been thoroughly fucked* hair? And, holy hell, was that a hickey on the side of my neck? I leaned over the sink and peered closer.

Damn it all. It was.

I tilted my head and twisted it this way and that. Hopefully, I'd be able to cover it with my hair and makeup. I touched it, not quite believing I had a hickey. Hell, I never had one in high school. I wasn't sure I wanted to go back to Boston tomorrow. I was damn sure I didn't want to go into the office.

But our flight left pretty early in the morning, if I remembered correctly, and it would look very strange if Tenor showed up at the office, which I was sure he would, and I didn't. There was no helping it, I had to go into the office tomorrow.

But the early flight did give me a reason not to crawl back into bed for round two with Tenor even though the mere thought of him had my traitorous body begging for more. I was a big girl; I had self-control. I could walk out of the bathroom, tell him goodnight and that I'd see him in the morning. Then I'd walk out the door and not look back.

I stood up and squared my shoulders. With a nod at myself in the mirror, I turned out the light and opened the door, fully prepared to be on my way.

Tenor stood at the foot of the bed, naked with his cock erect and ready. In his hands he held two glasses of wine. "Nightcap?"

I smiled and took one, crawling right back into bed with him.

Come to find out, I'm a bit lacking in the self-control department.

CHAPTER FIFTEEN

TENOR

*W*e almost missed our flight.

Somehow between the second glass of wine and our third round of sex, we fell asleep without setting an alarm or requesting a wakeup call. It was only because Sara received an alert that I had not checked in for the flight and called to make sure we were okay that we woke up at all.

While I answered the phone and assured her that yes, we were fine and that no, we'd make it to the airport on time, Mia was flying around throwing things haphazardly into suitcases. This was not how I'd planned for the morning to go. Not at all. I looked at her in longing, wishing for ten more minutes in bed, while at the same time, vividly remembering everything we'd done the night before.

"Why are you standing there? Get dressed," Mia shrieked at me. "The cab will be downstairs in five minutes and if we have any hope at all of making our flight, we have to leave as soon as it gets here, which means we should be already be waiting downstairs."

"Breathe, Mia." I grabbed a pair of jeans, knowing I'd have to stop at home to take a shower before heading into the office. Besides, it'd be better for both of us if we didn't arrive together. "We'll make our flight."

She glared at me and opened her mouth as if she was going to say something, but instead she threw her hair over her shoulder and stomped out. In the second before she turned, I caught a hint of color on her neck and groaned. Fuck. I'd given her a hickey.

I didn't want to make her any more upset than she already looked, so I threw on a tee shirt and hurriedly gathered everything else, making it into the hallway at the same time she did. We didn't speak, but thankfully we were alone on the elevator.

"I'm sorry about the..." I pointed to her neck. "I don't even remember doing that."

She stared straight ahead. "I'll find some way to ensure it stays hidden. Makeup. Hair. Something. I doubt I can get away with a scarf or turtleneck in this weather. I'll have to find something, or else I might as well pin a great red 'A' on my shirt and introduce myself as that girl who fucked the boss."

She sounded angry and I didn't know how to reply. It made me feel useless.

It was a feeling that didn't get any better even after we had got to the airport, or after we finally boarded our flight. I wasn't sure what to say. I wasn't going to apologize for the night before, because I wasn't sorry at all. Nor would I trivialize it, tell her that it was nothing. Nothing could have been further from the truth. On the other hand, I didn't want to make it sound like it was some beginning to a long-term romance or anything like that. In the end, I didn't do anything other than let her stew in her own emotions.

We parted ways at the airport. Before I left to get my car, I told her I would be in the office in a few hours. I didn't want to dictate when she should get in, but I wanted her to know she didn't have to check in right away.

However, if I thought the flight home was uncomfortable, as soon as I pulled into my driveway I knew the day wasn't going to get any better. Piers was waiting in his car for me.

I ignored him as I parked and made my way inside. Of course, he was right behind me. He didn't take long before getting to the point of his visit.

"Are you an idiot?" he asked.

"I don't know what you're talking about." I placed my suitcase on the bar in the kitchen, planning to take it upstairs after he left.

"Don't play stupid with me. I've known you too long and I can see right through you."

"Good," I said. "Do you see me giving you the bird, because I am."

"Damn it, Tenor. Act like an adult instead of a five-year-old."

If he only knew what very adult things I had been doing. "What brings you to my house today?" I asked him. "I've just returned from Atlanta where I was on a business trip and I'm a bit tired, but have to go by the office for a few hours, so if we could speed this along, I'd appreciate it."

"Did Mia accompany you to Atlanta?"

I stared at him and tried to figure out exactly what he was doing in my house. Not only that, but how he knew that I was on a business trip with Mia and that we had just returned. It wasn't like him to stop by unannounced like this. There was something more going on than what I could see. The fact that

Piers was involved only made it that much more ominous.

"Yes," I answered his question, looking for any hint to decipher what was really going on. "She did. Although, I don't understand what concern of yours it is. So before I answer more of your questions, you're going to answer one of mine. Why are you here?"

He placed his hands on top of the kitchen island and leaned forward. His face was flush and a vein in his neck pounded. I'd rarely seen him in such a state. "You fucked her, didn't you?"

"I'm not answering you. I don't see how it's any of your concern anyway."

"Oh, you don't, do you? I told you that if you were going to fuck her you should damn well do it before she became your employee." He pushed away from the island. "Damn it, Tenor, you never listen, do you? Is it even possible for you to make a decision without involving your dick? I certainly hope her pussy was worth it."

I took a deep breath and somehow managed not to hit him while doing so. "You're crossing the line. Watch yourself." I didn't like the way he spoke so disrespectful about her and I wouldn't put up with it for much longer.

"Watch myself? Are you serious? You want me to watch myself? Unfucking believable."

I wasn't going to remind him of all the times he screwed around and let his dick do the thinking for him. He would say it wasn't applicable to this circumstance and he would be right. Still, where did he get off talking like he was Mr. Perfect? I could've hit him for that remark about Mia and been totally justified in doing so. But there was that nagging voice that told me there was a hint of truth in what he said.

I hadn't given any thought to my company or my job or my responsibilities or anything like that the night before. Hell, I'd admitted as much to myself last night. Still, I thought there were something a bit more going on than him being upset I'd slept with Mia. I'd never seen Piers quite as livid before.

"It's not a big deal," I told him, though I wasn't sure if it was him I was truly trying to convince. "Mia's cool with it. She knows the score. Matter of fact, she told me she'd sign something if I wanted her to."

Piers ran his fingers through his hair which made it all messed up, sticking this way and that. If I hadn't been worried before, that would have done it. Piers never had a hair out of place. It didn't even look like him. "Mother fucking hell. Tell me she didn't say that."

I leveled my gaze at him. "Why don't you tell me exactly what's going on?"

"When you were in Atlanta, did you happen to meet a man by the name of Benjamin Douglas?"

I'd had that sinking feeling things were going to end up being worse than I thought when I walked in the door, never had I ever imagined hearing that name. "How do you know him?"

He didn't answer my question. Oh no, he had sensed the name Benjamin Douglas meant something to me and like a shark smelling blood, he wanted more. "Did you have a physical altercation with Mr. Benjamin Douglas while you were in Atlanta?"

My face must have revealed the truth before I could verbalize a response. Although I had to give it him, he took no pride in knowing how I'd answer.

"Fucking hell, Tenor," he said. "What have you gotten yourself into this time?"

"Tell me how you know that name." I pounded my fist on the island.

Realizing he wasn't getting any additional information without telling me something, he relented. "Mr. Douglas sent me an email this morning. In it he indicated that the night before last, you accosted him while he was on a date with Mia."

I snorted. "Accosted, my ass. He was assaulting her or getting ready to. However you want to put it, he was in her room, she asked him to leave, and he didn't, so I took care of it. I threw him out of her room, and yes, I may have been a little rough, but Mia was safe and I'd do it again the same way if I had the chance to do it over. Except I might actually hit him if given the chance."

Piers nodded as if he'd already heard the story. "Yes, he said that's the story you'd tell."

"Of course I would. It's what happened. What I don't understand is why he felt the need to send you an email only to say I was physical with him when he was clearly in the wrong." I didn't understand one damn thing about this entire conversation other than the fact that it was making me angry and I was about to lose my shit all over Piers.

"The thing is, Douglas claims it wasn't assault."

"Horse shit. I was there. I saw it. I heard it."

But Piers was shaking his head. "According to Douglas, it was consensual non-consent."

"What?"

"In the kink world it's when two or more people agree to engage in non-consent play. Some women

152

have rape fantasies. A scene like this would allow her a safe way to explore it."

"I know what consensual non-consent is, nimwit."

He held his hands up. "You asked what."

"As in, what the fuck?" I closed my eyes trying to calm down and make sense of what I'd just been told. I didn't believe it, not for one second. The memory of the fear in Mia's eyes and the way her body shook beside mine while we sat on the couch after, was too vivid and real. I opened my eyes and looked at Piers. "I don't believe it."

But as much as I didn't believe it was role play, it was obvious he did. "Douglas said she didn't tell you because she was embarrassed. Especially after you threw him out. She was afraid of what you'd think of her and that you wouldn't understand."

"I'm still not buying it. You don't get why because you didn't see her. I did. I was there. It was real." There was no part of me that could for one fraction of a second think she'd been acting.

"Maybe she's a really good actress," he said and before I could tell him no one was that good, he asked, "Have the two of you done any role play? I'm only asking to verify if it's something she's into."

It was one my lips to say 'no' when I had a flashback of Mia in the moonlight, her expression playful and her voice full of mischief as she asked, "Come here often?" But surely that didn't prove anything. "Come on," I said to him. "Be reasonable for just a minute. Do you know how many people role play? Seriously? If that's all you have, I can't believe they let you out of law school."

Piers wasn't backing down, not one little bit and the only possible reason as to why hit me with the force of a speeding train. He had more. *Fuck.*

"Hit me with the rest of it, Piers." I didn't want to hear anymore, but whatever it was had been important enough for him to make sure he was here when I arrived. And I had a bad feeling I hadn't heard the worst of it.

"Let's go sit down." Piers motioned toward my kitchen table.

"What the fuck's wrong with you? How old do you think I am, ninety? Tell me what else you have that is so important and so damning that you had to be waiting for me in my fucking driveway so you could attack me without even giving me a chance to put my suitcase down." I shouldn't have been mad at him, but unfortunately, he was the only one present at the moment, so he was the one who had to deal with my wrath.

"Mia told Douglas she knew you wanted to sleep with her and she didn't know how to get out of it." He was very calm as he spoke, eerily calm. "If you slept with her last night, I'm fairly certain it was a set up."

I froze in place. This was what happened when I acted without regard for my career and my company and the name I'd worked so hard to build. All those years of doing the right thing, saying the right thing, and for always standing firm, even when it was hard, all those years could so easily be wiped away with one bad decision. "Did he say what they wanted?" I asked, even though I still couldn't believe it to be a set up. Maybe if we'd only done it once, but I had her three times. Three.

"He hasn't made any demands yet, but I'm sure they'll be coming. He probably wanted to wait for her to get home." He took a deep breath. "I feel partially responsible. I never should have let you hire her. It was too much. How else could we have expected her to act when she had no other choice but to work for you?"

It made sense when I looked at it from that perspective. I'd taken away her business, her liveli-hood, shortly after her mother died. For the first time in her life she was alone and I'd done nothing but taken more away from her.

"I did think it was very strange that Benjamin Douglas just happened to show up right as we were checking in." Had she really faked the excitement when she saw him? Damn, she was an excellent actress, but I was still pissed that I hadn't been able to see through her. Not to mention, I was embarrassed she might have been faking with me. "What do we do now?"

Piers straightened his jacket. "*We* aren't going to do anything. *I'm* going to take care of this for you."

"No, I can't let you do that." It would be wrong of me to not talk to Mia and hear her side of the story. I owed her that much. No matter how convincing Piers sounded, I needed to see her eyes when I asked her. "Absolutely not."

"I think this is a mistake," he said. "You should let me take care of it."

"It's a mistake I made. I'll take care of it." But not today. Today the memory of the night before was too strong and I feared I wouldn't be able to be objective. I'd work from home the rest of the day and talk with Mia in the office first thing tomorrow. "I'll call you in the morning as soon as I talk with her."

He raised an eyebrow. "You're not going in today?"

"No, I don't think that would be the wisest thing for me to do."

"I understand." He paused for minute and then smiled. "Why don't you let me take you out to lunch? I feel bad for dropping this on you."

"No thanks. I appreciate the offer, but I'd be rotten company. And no need to apologize, I know you have my back. I'm grateful to have you on my side." Even so, I still let out a sigh of relief when he left.

Maybe in the silence of my house I could piece together what happened and locate at what point it went horribly bad.

CHAPTER SIXTEEN

MIA

Sara smiled brightly when I made it into the office two hours after landing. In those two hours, I'd showered, unpacked, and had an ugly cry. Not necessarily in that order. I'd also told myself that we were back in Boston and that meant not dwelling on what happened in Atlanta. Initially, I'd told myself I wouldn't even think about what happened in Atlanta, but that hadn't seemed reasonable or likely, so I'd settled on dwell.

"Is Mr. Butler in yet?" I asked her, while trying to act like my heart wasn't nearly pounding out of my chest at simply saying his name.

Her smile faltered. "No, he called about an hour ago and said he'd be working from home the rest of the day."

That fucker. "Really?" I asked, managing to keep the smile on my face. "I'll just call him there then."

I moved past her and into the hall that led to my office. All in all, I thought I handled my first encounter back in the office, post boss sex, very well. I recalled everything I said, my tone of voice, and body language, and decided there was nothing that even remotely suggested I'd left his bed hours ago.

I felt pretty good when I pushed open the door to my office and stepped inside. I froze, however, at the sight of the man sitting at my desk and looking for all the world as if he belonged there. At first sight, one would think he was comfortable and relaxed, however, the longer I looked at him, I saw it was only an act. He was only pretending to be at ease. There was a tremor of energy that ran through him he might think he hid, but it didn't work. At least not on me.

Only secondarily did I take in his looks. On another man, the nondescript brown hair and eyes would be considered unfortunate at best and boring at least. However, on him the features became striking and boring became anything but.

"Hello, Mia," he said, proving it was my office he intended to be. I tried to place his slight accent, but failed. "I'm Piers Worthington, Bachelor

International's head of legal counsel. Why don't you close the door so we can talk privately?"

Legal counsel? My brain threatened to short circuit. "I'd rather keep it open if it's all the same with you."

He shrugged. "It's completely up to you. I thought you might not want the rest of the office to hear about how you and Mr. Butler spent your time in Atlanta."

I stood dumbstruck. Did Tenor call his legal counsel first thing when he walked in the door to his house? I couldn't believe it. There was no way. Unless... this Piers guy wasn't talking about Tenor and I having sex after all.

I worked to keep my voice steady, even though inside I was shaking. "Mr. Butler and I did a lot of things in Atlanta. You'll have to be a bit more specific."

"Before he hired you, I advised Mr. Butler that if he wanted to fuck you that he do it before you signed the employment contract." Piers' expression showed no emotion. "It didn't happen that way, did it, Mia?"

I turned around and shut the office door. Tenor had told him. Not only had he told him and not only was it one of the first things he did when he arrived home, but he didn't even have the courage to come in and face me. Damn his lying, good for nothing, ass. He sent his lawyer to do his dirty work. How had I so badly misjudged him?

"What do you want Mr. Worthington?" I asked him, even though I really didn't want to know.

"I want what I've always wanted, Mia. Whatever is best for Mr. Butler and his business interests." He smile was fake, I could see right through it.

"I fail to see how that has anything to do about our time in Atlanta."

"I know about Benjamin Douglas," he said as if that explained everything. All it really did was confuse me more. But when I started to say something, he held up a hand to stop me. "Let me talk for a few minutes. You see, you and I are a lot alike. In fact, between the three of us, you and I are a lot more alike than Tenor is to either one of us. You and I didn't grow up the way he did. We weren't born into a wealthy lifestyle. We weren't given the best of everything growing up. We had to work and fight for every little thing, didn't we?"

I had no idea where this conversation was going and I knew nothing about this Piers guy, other than he seemed like a dick. I wasn't about to engage in this conversation. I remained silent, but stood where I was and crossed my arms over my chest so I wouldn't hit him, and waited for him to continue. I tapped my foot, each tap a second closer to the time I could tell him to get the hell out of my office.

"A person who grows up like that is very different than a person who grows up like Tenor," he continued on, not minding that I'd ignored his question. "Tenor sees things differently than you and I do. He'll never understand why you acted the way you did."

The way I acted when? I wanted to ask, but the entire conversation dumbfounded me.

"But I get you. I do. And I understand why you did it. Because of that, I'm going to do something for you that Tenor never would."

"I have no idea what you're talking about," I said, glad that I had finally found my voice.

"Come on, Mia. You can drop the innocent lines with me. I know everything. He told me." His tone was gentler now. He wanted me to trust him.

Fat chance.

"Tenor?" I asked, even though I didn't know who else he'd be talking about.

"No. Not Tenor. I know about the plans you made with Benjamin Douglas."

I shivered remembering his rough hands on me

and my voice was small when I replied. "I still don't know what you're talking about."

"There's no reason to hide the truth from me. I've already told you I understand. Frankly, I think just about anyone in your situation would do the same thing." His voice was soothing as if he wanted to put me at ease, but it wasn't genuine. His tone smacked of insincerity, no matter what he tried to convince me otherwise. "You lost your mother and business partner. Then you find out she had taken a sizable loan from one of your competitors." He shook his head. "It's a vexing situation to find yourself in."

"I still don't—"

"Stop." He interrupted. "I'm letting you out of your contract."

He paused, obviously expecting me to say something, but I had no words.

"The agreement is this: You are released from the requirement to work for Tenor. In addition, I make the quarter of a million go away. You have ten thousand in your bank account. My recommendation is that you use it to get out of Boston. Go somewhere new. Make a new start."

He made it sound so tempting. But nothing came without a cost. I didn't know what to do. I needed to talk to Tenor, but that seemed less and less likely. It was too hard to think at the moment. "What do I have to do in order for this to happen?"

"Simple." He smiled. "You stay away from Tenor. You leave him alone and that means Douglas does as well."

"What's in this for you?" I asked because I knew he had to be getting something. He wasn't doing this for completely altruistic reasons and I'd yet to figure out how Benjamin played into all of this.

"Bachelor International is safe," he said. "But most important, Tenor is safe. He's one of the few remaining gentlemen and I don't like to see him taken advantage of."

Every word that came out of Piers' mouth did nothing but add to my confusion and anger. According to him, I was nothing more than a scam artist, always looking for my next target. "This deal makes it sound like I'm guilty of something and I'm not. What if I don't take it?" I asked.

"I don't suggest that."

"I didn't think you would and that wasn't my question."

"If you don't sign, I will make sure you wished you had. Remember when I said I grew up the same as you?" He waited for my nod before answering. "Growing up I met a lot of different people. Not all of them were model citizens then and they are even less so today. I'm still in contact with a good number of them. They aren't the type of people you'd like to meet alone, if you know what I mean."

His voice was still just as calm as it had always been. It was a bit unnerving for him to be so calm when I was anything but. Especially after that last statement. He didn't say anything else, just raised his eyebrow. I swallowed hard. "Are you threatening me?"

"Absolutely not. The only thing I'm doing is telling you what will happen if you don't take the deal."

"It sorta sounds like the same thing from where I'm standing," I said with a lot more calm than I felt. I didn't know what to think or what to do. And for the first time in my life I didn't have anyone to ask for help.

What made Tenor change his mind from the short period of time from his bedroom to his house? And even then, why did he first go to his lawyer instead of coming to me? A hundred other similar questions ran through my head. Like how did Benjamin Douglas fit into this conversation? Piers shouldn't even know the man's name. Unfortunately, no matter what the question was, the detail that laid the foundation for the problem never changed: Tenor didn't want me anymore. Not just working for his business, not just in his bed, but he didn't want any kind of relationship with me.

My chest tightened and it hurt. It hurt so bad. But what hurt the most was, in the end the decision was made for me. If he had been at least willing to talk to me, I'd be willing to try to stick it out and uphold my end of the contract. But what viable option did I have other than to take Piers' offer?

I took a deep breath. "I don't feel as if I have a choice in this matter."

Piers templed his fingers on my desk. "Don't be dramatic, Mia. You always have a choice. No, you don't have to take my offer, but let's not forget, it was your choices that put you in this position in the first place."

Not totally true, I wanted to argue. Mama had made the choice to involve Tenor without even asking my opinion in the matter. I didn't tell Piers any of that, though, because one, it was my mother and two, she was dead. It didn't seem fair to lay all the blame at her feet with her not able to defend herself.

"Fine," I told Piers and suddenly my legs were wobbly and I'd give anything to crawl back into bed.

Probably mostly due to only having two hours of sleep the night before, but I refused to think about that right now. Especially with Piers in the room. "Just tell me what I need to do so I can get out of here and try to pretend as if the last few weeks haven't happened."

CHAPTER SEVENTEEN

TENOR

*I*t took damn near all night but by the time the sun came up I had a workable plan, or at least, I hoped it was. I hurried through getting dressed, wanting to get to the office before Mia did.

My plan was to go into her office as soon as she arrived, close the door, and have a long talk about the allegations Piers had been all too happy to throw her way. The fact that I thought she was innocent would carry zero weight. I needed to talk to Mia in order to try and understand what the hell Benjamin Douglas thought he was doing.

Sara wasn't at her desk when I walked into the office, but that wasn't surprising since I was so early.

I stopped by the break room to make some coffee before I started my wait for Mia.

Three hours later she still hadn't arrived. Deep inside I knew something was wrong an hour and a half into my wait, but I decided to give her a little more time. When I could no longer pretend everything was okay, I walked back to the front to Sara's desk.

She gave me a tentative smile. "Good morning, Mr. Butler, is there something I can help you with?"

"Yes, you can. Did Mia come in yesterday?"

She looked at him strangely, as if I'd asked her if she lived on Earth. "Yes, Mr. Butler," she answered, but it sounded like she'd had to keep herself from adding, "Duh."

"Was she sick or did she say anything about not coming in today?"

Again with the look like I'd asked the most preposterous question ever. "I have to be honest, sir. No one expected her back."

I tilted my head trying to understand how what she said could possibly be a viable answer to my question. "What?"

"It was an assumption on our part when Mr. Worthington walked her out and she was carrying her stuff in a box."

"He what?" My body shook as if it'd already comprehended what Sara was saying.

She looked at me in confusion. "Mr. Worthington was waiting in Mia's office when she arrived yesterday afternoon. They stayed in there with the door closed for some time, and when they came out, she had a box of her things and he walked her out. Neither one of them have been back since then, sir. You didn't know about this?"

Finally, I could at least understand why Sara was confused. How would it be possible in her mind for her employer, who was also the business owner, not to know his legal counsel had fired an employee? The words rang in my head and I had to clear them from my mind so I could think. Without answering Sara, I went back to my desk long enough to grab my keys and then left the office.

I had given only a fleeting thought to either calling Piers or demanding that he meet me. Neither of those would work, I realized almost instantaneously, because they would give him time to prepare and I wanted him completely off guard. Or as off guard as possible. Surely, he knew he'd have to face me eventually.

I drove to his office building, near the harbor, the overly congested roads doing nothing to soothe my temper. I pulled into the parking lot and quickly located his car, a racy little thing that would smash him like a bug if he ever got into an accident. Lucky for him I wasn't able to park beside it. The exterior was far too perfect, I thought, and would look much better with a ding or five.

His office was on the top floor and the smile his own admin had for me quickly dissolved when she looked me over. I realized I had both hands curled into fists and I slowly released them.

"Mr. Worthington is meeting with a client, Mr. Butler," she said, standing, but wisely not blocking me from the door.

"Then I suggest you call and let him know it's over, because I'm going in and no one is going to stop me." I didn't wait for her reply, because honestly, it didn't matter to me one way or the other what she thought about me breaking up his meeting.

When I found him, however, he wasn't in his conference room with a client, he was standing just outside his doorway. Almost as if he was waiting for me.

"Tenor," he said. "I've been expecting you. Come on in."

We walked inside his office and he closed the door, but neither one of us sat down. It became very obvious, very quickly that he was not going to say anything before I did. That was fine with me. I had plenty of things to say to him.

"What the hell did you do, Piers?" I asked him.

He didn't answer right away, but calmly walked over to his desk and sat down. "I took care of a problem that you refused to."

I shoved the papers off his desk and leaned in. "What did you do to her? What did you say? Where is she?"

"I don't know why you're so taken by that little thief. Trust me, you and your business are so much better without her. You should be thanking me instead of storming in here like a mad man. Although," he stopped to briefly touch his fingertip to his lips. "She never once admitted anything. In fact, she was still proclaiming her innocence when she started her car and drove away."

I saw white spots dance before me. "Maybe because she is innocent, asshole. Did that thought ever cross your mind?"

He shook his head. "You should have seen her face when I mentioned Benjamin Douglas. She's not innocent."

"That wasn't guilt, you bastard, it was fear. He tried to assault her."

"Don't call me that," he said and I was glad to finally hear a little bit of emotion in his voice, but only because of the name I'd called him. Not because he felt bad about anything he'd done. "And I believe I already went over the consent thing."

I wasn't going to go over semantics with him right now. There would be time for that later. "Tell me what you told her to make her leave."

"I paid her off. Told her the loan would be forgiven if she left and didn't come back."

Anger raged inside me. "That wasn't your deal to make."

"And yet I did." His tone was unapologetic, almost provoking, and his unasked question lingered in the air. *And just what are you going to do about it?*

"You're fired," I said. "As of right now, you no longer work for me and therefore, you are to have nothing to do with anything related to me or my business."

"You can't fire me," he said, and his untouchable facade broke just a bit.

I kept my eyes on my best friend since forever so he'd know I meant every word I said. "And yet I did." I walked out of his office without looking back.

CHAPTER EIGHTEEN

MIA

"What are you doing here this time of day?" Wren asked when I knocked on her door late in the morning the day after Piers fired me.

"I brought your dress back." I held up the dress I'd worn out to dinner with Tenor and tried not to think about how it felt when he took it off or what we did after. It didn't work, my hands shook.

"Did he like it? Shouldn't you be at work?" she asked. "And what's wrong? Did something happen in Atlanta? You don't look so good." She didn't take the dress back to her room, but hanged it in her home office. I took a seat on the couch next to her desk.

"Which question do you want me to answer

first?" I asked, surprising myself with how weak my voice was.

She bit her bottom lip and shook her head, which confirmed what I'd thought this morning when I got out of bed after getting less than an hour of sleep: I looked like hell warmed over. It didn't appear as if she was going to reply, so I took a deep breath and answered, "I thought he liked it. Yes, normally I would be at work, but Tenor's legal guy fired me for him."

"What?" Wren croaked.

I had planned to answer the rest of her questions, but that had been the first time I'd voiced what happened the day before and it hurt so much more than I'd thought it would to say the words. The tears started silently, but once they did start, they wouldn't stop and within minutes, I found myself sobbing uncontrollably.

Wren, being the friend that she was, didn't say anything, but sat beside me and let me cry. I'm not sure how long I sat there on her couch and cried, but when I finally stopped, her eyes were wet and red as well.

She squeezed my hand and I hadn't even real-ized she'd been holding it. "Tell me everything," she said. "Don't leave anything out."

I ended up telling her everything. From arriving in the lobby and the horrible date with Benjamin, to the great meetings the next day and the wonderful date with Tenor that followed. I didn't tell her all the details surrounding what happened once we returned to the hotel, but enough that she knew the trip had not been platonic.

When I finished, I felt twenty pounds lighter. It felt so good to unload and lean on another person. Plus, Wren was also an investigative journalist. While I knew that as my best friend, she wouldn't be able to be completely objective, she might be able to shed some light on potentially important details I'd overlooked or offer some insight I hadn't considered before.

But she didn't say anything right away and as the silence continued I began to worry. I worried that she thought less of me or that she judged me. I almost got up and apologized for coming by and inter-rupting her own work time, but then she spoke.

"I don't see how it was possible for Tenor to get in touch with his attorney, bring him up to speed on everything that went on in Atlanta, and have him go wait in your office so he could fire you." She thought a little bit more and then asked, "Did he talk on the phone at any time yesterday morning or did you see him get wifi on the plane?"

"No to either of those," I said, wondering why I didn't take notice of the short time Tenor would have to set in motion what happened at the office yesterday. "But assuming that's what happened, why would Piers fire me? And how and why would he do so without Tenor's consent?"

It sounded good, but no matter how badly I wanted it to be true, I couldn't work it out in my mind to make it so. Other than the one overwhelming truth - nothing about what had happened matched Tenor's character.

"Ask yourself this," Wren said. "Does the way Piers portrayed Tenor yesterday jive with any part of his personality?"

"No," I answered, pleased she'd been thinking the same. I had to admit Tenor wasn't afraid of doing hard or even unpopular things. And he wasn't the sort to let others do his dirty work. In fact, in the short time I'd known him, I'd never seen or heard of him backing away from a challenge. The more thought of it, the less and less anything that happened yesterday matched any piece of the man I knew him to be. "But why would Piers fire me so suddenly like that and how does Benjamin fit in?"

"I don't get those parts either," she admitted. "It doesn't make any sense why he would do something like that out of the blue."

"He wouldn't do it out of the blue," I said. "And the fact that he did, especially if he did it without Tenor's knowledge, makes me think he believes he knows something Tenor doesn't."

"What could that possibly be?"

"I have no idea." I tapped the toe of my shoe on the floor. "I can only hope that when Tenor finds out, he calls me."

Surely he would. Wouldn't he talk to me regardless of whether or not Piers initiated it? If he hadn't gone by the office yesterday, like Sara said, he might not have found out until this morning when he got in. Which meant maybe he would call me today. Or maybe he would go a step further and come by my apartment.

"Mia?" Wren asked.

"I should hear from him today, don't you think?" I stood to my feet, perhaps I'd go to him.

"If you really want my opinion, I'll give it to you," she said, and when I didn't object, she continued, "If I were you, I'd have called him last night to ask what the hell was going on."

I could see her doing exactly that. In fact, had the

tables been reversed, it's the same advice I'd have given her. I had thought about calling him last night. The only thing that kept me from doing it was the fact that he'd been behind the whole thing. But now that I'd talked it through with Wren, that seemed less and less likely.

"You're right," I told her, walking to the door. "I'm going to go make myself look decent and then I'm going to go see him."

She walked with me to my car. When we reached it, she gave me a hug. "Go get him and call me when you find out what happened."

I'm sure I broke a good number of traffic laws as I drove back to my apartment. In my head I ran through several potential conversations we could have. Would he be despondent? Angry with Piers? Would he ask me to come back to work for him and if so, how would I answer?

One of my conditions to Piers the day before was that I didn't want Mama's debt erased. It wasn't right for Piers to do that to Tenor and I didn't agree with it. I'd made that perfectly clear to Piers, but whether that information was relayed to Tenor, I wasn't sure. Come hell or high water, and if I had to live on rice and beans for five years, so be it, but one day I would pay back every cent we owed Tenor, with interest.

Hell, if I had to put it in my will, I'd do it.

I immediately noticed the *much too expensive for this neighborhood* car in my apartment's parking area, but I didn't look to see who was in it because I feared it wasn't Tenor and equally feared it was. What would I say to him if it was him? Even if it wasn't, I still needed to figure it out since I would be talking with him at some point during the day.

I pulled into a free spot, glad that whoever it was had parked far enough away for me to make it inside without them catching up to me. A car door closed behind me as I unlocked the front door. I didn't look over my shoulder to see who it was. If it was someone for me, I'd find out soon enough. If it wasn't, it didn't matter.

The door wasn't closed any longer than ten seconds before someone knocked though. I didn't have time to make it upstairs to my apartment. I repeated to myself I could do this. That I was strong enough to look him in the eye and have the necessary conversation. But then he called my name and knees threatened to give out.

"Mia!" he shouted almost desperately.

I didn't answer because I was trying to deal with the fact that Tenor was right outside the front door. I opened my mouth, but nothing came out.

"Mia!"

"Coming," I said, but it came out in a whisper and I was positive he didn't hear.

"I know you're there," he said, obviously thinking I was refusing to see him as opposed to working up the nerve to face him. "I just saw you enter."

I had been called many things in my life and I was sure I'd be called a lot more before it was all said and done, but I'd never been called a coward and I wasn't going to start then. It'd take more than Tenor Butler to make a stand in the foyer of my apartment building and pretend not to hear someone beating the door down and yelling my name so loud that Ms. Hopper, a first floor resident, who was deaf, could hear him.

I flung the door open and stared at wide blue eyes of Tenor Butler. "Mia," he said.

"Yes," I replied, finding no trace of the woman who'd cried her eyes out earlier. "And I'm not sure why you're surprised about that. I mean, I'm assuming you knew it was me, since you appear to have driven yourself here and you were calling my name a few seconds ago."

"I'm sorry," he said and there was no deceit in his eyes.

"About which part?"

"May I come in?" he asked instead of answering my question.

"Only if you agree to answer any questions I have and tell me the truth, the whole truth, and nothing but the truth."

"So help me, God," he finished with a smile, but obviously my expression showed I wasn't anywhere near close enough to joke. "Sorry."

He ran a hand through his hair and I moved a step over and opened the door a bit so he could walk in. We didn't talk as I led him up the stairs to my apartment and eventually to my living area, where we sat down on a couch. He sat as far away as he could and still be on the couch himself.

All the questions I had for him ran through my mind and I summed them all up in one. "What the hell, Tenor?"

He shifted in his seat, but the look in his eyes radiated anger and not guilt. "I didn't know until I went into the office this morning and you never showed up. I asked Sara. She told me about Piers."

I didn't feel as much relief as I thought I would hearing him say that. It confirmed I'd drawn the right conclusion, but I still had so many questions. "Why would Piers even think about doing something like that without your permission?"

A muscle in his jaw ticked. "Benjamin Douglas sent him an email claiming the two of you had masterminded a plan to set me up for a sexual harassment lawsuit."

"What the hell?" I said, because there was no way he'd just said what I thought he had.

But Tenor was nodding. "He went so far as to confess that what I walked into was nothing more than a consensual, non-consent scene."

Hot rage raced throughout my body and my throat tightened, making it difficult to speak. "I'll find him and rip his dick off." It seemed as good as a place to start as any. "I can't believe I told you not to go after him and break his nose."

He let his breath out in a sigh. "I thought that same thing."

"And Piers just blindly trusted him? How is that possible?" I asked, my voice rising.

He shook his head. "Apparently, his email was quite convincing."

I wasn't sure what surprised me more, that Benjamin would send an email like that or that someone would actually believe it. "But not so convincing that you would believe it?"

"No," he said. "Which is probably why he sent it to Piers and not to me."

"Holy shit," I said, because the more I thought about, the more pissed I became. My cheeks felt hot and I knew they were red.

"I fired him as soon as I found out what he did," Tenor said.

"You fired Piers?" I wrinkled my eyebrows. "But you two have been friends since preschool."

"A true friend would have never done what he did."

While I agreed with him in principle, I didn't like being the issue that divided two friends. Tenor would always see me as the girl he lost his best friend over. I feared that if we continued down our present path, Tenor would wind up resenting me. Maybe not today or tomorrow, but one day he would and as bad as the last twenty-four hours had been, they would pale in comparison to the day he looked at me with guilt and regret.

I didn't say anything at first because I knew he'd argue with me. If I knew him like I thought I did, he would be totally convincing and I'd end up agreeing with him. Before Tenor decided to get on a white horse and feel compelled to rescue me, I needed to set a few things straight.

"Piers went about it all wrong," I said, digging to find the strength to say the words that needed to be said. "But I don't think it's a good idea for us to work together. More to the point, I don't think it's a good idea for me to work for you."

He didn't argue with me and that came as a shock. Apparently he didn't think we should work together either. He looked down to the floor. I had to admit, that hurt, even though it didn't make sense since I felt the same. He sighed. "I know, and I happen to agree. I should never have let things go as far as they did in Atlanta."

I snorted, because really, how much further could we have gone?

"I've never acted so inappropriately with an employee before and it was disrespectful of me to do so with you."

He said it so matter of factly, it kind of pissed me off. "It wasn't only you there, you know. I was an active participant and I never told you to stop."

"I do know, yes, and as your employer, I shouldn't have had to rely on you to stop it. It should have never gotten to the point where there was anything to stop."

I didn't like the guilt in his voice. Part of me wanted to ask him if we were still seeing each other, but then I wasn't sure how to define "seeing". I was fairly certain "seeing" someone didn't always equate to getting naked.

"I don't know where we go from here," I confessed, but not able to look at him.

"I was thinking if you were a partner—"

"Stop, Tenor." I held my hand up. "Stop it right there. How in the world can I possibly be a partner when I owe you a quarter of a million dollars?"

"Piers said he forgave the loan yesterday," Tenor said.

"I'm sure to you that response makes all the sense in the world, but are you kidding me?" Surely he saw what I was talking about.

"What?" he asked, wrinkling his forehead.

"I need you to explain to me how this situation with Piers is going to work because sitting here I get confused." As soon as the words left my mouth, I knew he didn't get it. Not at all. And as much as I'd been hoping to talk without mentioning Piers, it appeared Fate had different plans. I took a deep breath. "Unfortunately for you, I don't think you can pick and choose what you like about the things Piers did yesterday. You can't ignore the fact that he fired me while at the same time agree that what he did with the loan is acceptable."

"Why not?"

"You just can't."

"And this entire time, I thought being able to do whatever I wanted to was one of the perks of being the owner and boss of the business," he spoke calmly, but I sensed the anger under the surface.

"Didn't Piers tell you that I was adamant about paying the loan back?" I felt my own anger rise.

"No, but to be fair, I really didn't give him much of a chance to say anything before I fired him."

I nodded as if I understood exactly what he was saying, but in reality, my heart was breaking because he'd just confirmed what I feared. From my point of view, the words *fair* and *Piers* should never be used in the same sentence. The man had fired me without cause and without the knowledge of Tenor. He didn't have the right to be treated fairly.

The fact that Tenor acted like it was no big deal he hadn't been told about me repaying the loan was all I needed to know. He may have fired Piers this morning, but I'd bet anything he'd be rehired within a week.

I didn't say any of this out loud, but I must have made some sort of negative facial expression, because Tenor didn't look quite as calm or at ease as he had moments prior. "You won't come back and work with me as a partner," he said, his voice flat. "And I'm hoping I'm wrong, but I have a feeling you won't go out with me anymore either."

I shook my head. Suddenly, I ached all over. I had nothing else to give him. "I can't, Tenor. Maybe if we had met a different way or something..." I let the sentence go unfinished and though neither of us said anything, the air between us felt heavy with the weight of impossible "what ifs".

"Well," he said, finally, and stood up. "If you ever change your mind. About either."

I won't, I wanted to say, but didn't. "I know how to get in touch."

He gave me a weak smile. "I'll always answer the phone when you call."

I don't know why hearing him say that made me feel like crying, but it did. "Thanks," I managed to get out, blinking back tears.

"I'll show myself to the door." He took a step toward me and for a second I thought he would kiss me, but then the second was gone and he'd moved away. He looked back once and then he walked out of the room. I waited until the door closed before allowing my tears to fall.

CHAPTER NINETEEN

MIA

$\mathcal{A}$ week later I was once again in my living room, but this time with Wren. She insisted on stopping by every other day even though I told her I was fine. This time she'd gone a step further and brought pizza with her. And not just any pizza, but a pie from our favorite Little Italy hang out. She said it was because she didn't eat lunch and for once I couldn't argue because she often skipped meals.

She claimed that sometimes she got so caught up in what she was doing, she'd forget to eat. I always thought it had more to do with the years she spent training in ballet and less to do with getting lost in her work. Either way, there was little to no chance of me ever forgetting a meal.

"What are you working on?" she asked, after finishing her third slice. "More consulting jobs?"

I had yet to take a permanent position anywhere, even though I'd been offered several. I would normally be flattered, but I had a feeling those were more as a result of Tenor making calls than anything else. I had to admit I thought it was sweet of him, but I wasn't looking for anything permanent. However, a few had been receptive when I'd suggested working as an ad hoc consultant.

"No, not tonight." I put down the financials and spreadsheets I'd been reviewing and reached for a slice of pepperoni, olives, and mushrooms. "I've been going through the records Mom had on the business."

"Have you found anything?"

"It's more like what I haven't found." I'd retraced Mom's footprints through several years of bank statements, bills, and delinquency notifications. "The loan allowed her to pay back all of her outstanding debt."

I knew this because I'd painstakingly gone through every transaction I could find and matched up the amount owed to the amount paid. I'd discovered early in the process to remove myself emotionally because otherwise, there was no way I'd get through it all.

"And something's not adding up?" Wren's eyes lit up and she was practically drooling to get her hands on the files. There was little she loved more than a puzzle. That was one of the reasons she'd done so well as an investigative journalist—she refused to stop until she had an answer.

"I can't match up one check with an invoice or bill."

"Just one?" She peered over my shoulder. "I'd say that's pretty damn impressive."

"One fifty-thousand-dollar check."

She nearly choked on her pizza. "Fifty?"

"Yes." I took a bite of my slice and closed my eyes. Nothing was better than fresh from the brick oven pizza. "I think I should put in a brick oven in my kitchen. Would that be odd?"

"Very. Can you tell who the check is to or for what?" she asked all businesslike.

"That's another issue. I can't find a copy of the cashed check anywhere. The bank doesn't even have it." I watched as she went over everything I said. It was fascinating to observe her work.

"Strange."

"Right?" I sighed. "I don't know what to do to move forward."

I'd thought about ignoring the fifty thousand, but I knew I wouldn't be able to. One way or the other, I would find out who the check was made to and why.

"If you need my help, let me know."

"I will. I promise."

There was one question I knew she wanted to ask and, to be honest, I was surprised she'd held out as long as she had without asking. I decided to throw her a bone. "I haven't heard from him in a week. What do you make of that?"

"Easy. He's giving you space and you know what happened the last time he did that?" She wiggled her eyebrows and it looked so funny, I had to laugh.

"Yes, well, that was then and this is now. And there is no way I'm stepping one foot inside his office." Though everyday the thought tempted me.

"You don't have to stop by his office. Take baby steps. Send him a text first."

Listening to her made it sound so easy. *Send him a text.* Yeah, like it was that simple. She didn't know how many times during the last week I'd pulled up his contact information and thought about doing that very thing.

Or the numerous times I'd catch myself

wondering what he was doing at that very moment. I told myself it was only normal, but I wasn't sure I completely believed that. No, I feared the truth was I'd fallen hard and fast for Tenor Butler and there would be no easy way to get over him. Even worse, I saw no way to work out being with him. Not with how I felt unequal beside him. He didn't see it that way, but I did which made it my issue to get over.

I just didn't know how.

I also wondered if he'd mended the fence with Piers. Then I'd secretly hoped he hadn't. Of course, that only made me feel worse, because what sort of person was I that I didn't want Tenor and his best friend to work things out?

But I confessed none of this to Wren. I didn't want her to know that I feared I was helplessly in love with my ex-boss, and that I was a horrible person as well. Though I had a feeling she knew about helplessly in love bit.

She grew very quiet as we finished dinner. It wasn't like her, but I figured she was just thinking about an article or something. "I'm going to tell you something," she said once the pizza was gone. Her tone was a combination of heartache and regret and so unlike her my mouth nearly gaped in shock when I turned and saw a lone tear slide down her cheek.

"Wren?"

"I don't talk about it but I've been where you are." Her smile was sad. "Most days I'm still there, if I'm honest."

"Italy?"

She nodded and wiped her nose. "God, it's been five years. You'd think I'd be over him."

Him. The man whose existence I'd suspected, but had never had proof of. The man who may or may not have been involved in whatever accident killed her dancing dream, but who for damn sure was responsible for the sadness my friend carried.

"We met my first day in the country and hit it off immediately." As she spoke, it was almost as if I saw her mind travel back to that country and time. "He was young and handsome and charming. Everything was so perfect, I kept telling myself it couldn't be real."

But it had been real. I could tell simply by looking at her how real it had been.

"We had almost a week together before I found out the truth about him," she said.

"What was the truth?" I asked after she didn't say anything.

"That he was only using me to get into the States. That he was a known playboy who never went out with the same woman twice." She looked at me and blinked a few tears out of the way. "I'd heard that last part before. I wasn't totally naive. But he managed to convince me that I was different. That he felt differently about me. Then one afternoon, almost two weeks after our arrival, I saw proof that he'd been lying to me. Forty-eight hours and too many drinks to count later, I woke up in an Italian hospital with two broken legs and no memory of how they got that way."

"Jesus, Wren." I felt as if the floor had disappeared beneath my feet. I'd never heard exactly what happened while she was in Italy, and even though I'd known it wouldn't be pretty, I had no idea just how horrible it had been.

"He came by the hospital a few times while I was there, but I told the nurses I didn't want to see him and they kept him away from me."

I couldn't imagine what had been like for her going through everything alone, in a strange country where she knew very little of the language and even fewer people.

"Oh, Wren," I said taking her hand and giving it a squeeze. "I wish I'd been there for you. It must have been horrible."

She gave my hand a slight squeeze back. "I wish

you had been there, too. And I wish I'd told you sooner, but I knew it'd hurt. And it does, but it feels good to finally get it out there."

I had so many questions to ask her, but I held back, at least for now, because I knew she'd had a reason for bringing up today what happened in Italy all those years ago.

"I wanted you to know there's not a day that goes by I don't wish I had let him come in to see me. Just once. That I'd allowed myself a bit of closure. But I didn't and now it's too late." Her eyes begged me. "Don't do like me. This thing you have with Tenor, it's real and different. I can see it, even if you won't admit it."

I took a shaky breath. "I have no problem admitting it," I told her. "It just doesn't matter one way or the other."

"I think you're wrong, but I'm not going to argue with you. Bottom line is, there's unfinished business between the two of you. You both need to sit down and sort it out or else you'll spend the rest of your life wishing you had."

I sat there for several long seconds and wondered when my friend had become so smart. My head knew she was correct, even if my heart wanted to deny it for a bit longer. "I can't promise you I'll see him again," I told her. "And I won't lie and tell you otherwise. However, I do promise that I'll think long and hard over what you've told me. *And* that I'll give serious thought to contacting Tenor."

"Thank you," she said. Suddenly she got a huge grin on her face and I couldn't help it. I grinned right back at her.

"What?"

"You should always take my advice, Ms. Smarty Pants Matchmaker. I'm pretty good at this relationship stuff. Except, you know, when it comes to my own. *That* I suck at. But I'm totally right about you and Tenor."

I flipped her the bird because she was still grinning. That only caused her to break out into laughter, so I threw a pillow from the couch at her and we both dissolved into giggles.

Two DAYS LATER, I was still searching online records looking for the fifty thousand I couldn't put my fingers on. I tapped my pen on top of the kitchen table. I was baffled and more than a little perturbed I wasn't able to find it because I knew it had to be somewhere. Seriously, it was right in front of me and somehow, I kept overlooking it.

The front door buzzer rang and I gladly closed the spreadsheets, thrilled to have something else to focus on. The number of people stopping by had decreased dramatically. If I had to guess, I'd guess it was an old friend of mama's stopping by to make sure I was getting along okay. A visit from one of her friends would nice.

As I walked across the floor, my phone rang. I assumed it was another matchmaking agency wanting me to do some consulting work for them and decided to let it go to voicemail. I made a mental note to call and thank Tenor for all the work he was sending my way.

"Hello," I said, using the intercom to connect with whoever buzzed my apartment.

"Mia Matthews," someone said in a voice I didn't recognize. I realized that not only was this person not one of mother's friends, but that he was also male.

"Yes," I answered hesitantly. I couldn't very well tell them that I was not, after all. They had come to my apartment. However, it felt a bit odd confirming such over an intercom.

"I'm from David and Daniels," he said, naming one of the most high-powered law offices in the city.

My first thought was, *holy shit, what had Piers done now?* I was getting ready to tell him to go jump when he spoke again.

"I'm sorry to disturb you, but it's about Ophelia Tuckerman."

Opa? I couldn't even begin to imagine why someone would come by my apartment for her, but it wasn't Piers and didn't sound like anything he had orchestrated, so I pushed the button to let the gentleman up.

My confusion hadn't abated even after I let him in.

"Jacob Evans," he said, reaching out for my hand. He had a briefcase in his other one. He appeared to be in his mid-fifties, his suit was well made, and his shoes didn't look as if they typically spent their day making house calls around the city.

"Have a seat, Mr. Evans." I pointed to the couch. "May I get you something to drink?"

He took a seat and placed the briefcase on the floor. "No, thank you. This shouldn't take very long."

I sat down. "You said this was about Opa?" I used her nickname intentionally because I remembered how much she disliked her full name.

He must have known that as well because he smiled, though I got the impression he was smiling at something else and not necessarily at me. "Yes," he said. "Typically, I'd have called you to my office for reading a will, but in this case, it seemed a bit overboard since it only concerns you."

I almost missed the "only concerns you" part because my brain kind of fizzled after he said, "reading a will."

"I...what?" I sputtered out.

He opened the briefcase and pulled out a stack of papers. "Ms. Tuckerman was the lone heir of David Tuckerman and she was her parents' only child. She never married because she said men only wanted her for her money, and she never had any children. She lived a modest life, but she was extremely generous when it came to charitable giving. Her original intentions had been to give away most of her wealth before she died, but a few years ago, she changed her mind. She came to me and said she was finished with the charities. Whatever was left, she wanted it put aside for you."

"Me? Why?" It was the most absurd thing I'd ever heard and I half expected him to bust out laughing and shout, "Fooled ya!"

Except he didn't. "Ms. Tuckerman said you and your mother were the two dearest friends she'd had. She said your mother told her that her one regret was not being able to give you everything you deserved. This is Ms. Tuckerman's way of fixing that."

He pulled more paper out of the briefcase at his side. "I'm afraid that up until she changed her wishes, we'd done a great job giving money away for her." He grimaced. "As of this morning, the estate is worth around four hundred seventy-five thousand dollars."

My jaw dropped, and I didn't seem to be able to close it, though I somehow managed to chant, "Oh, my God," several times.

"And," he said. "There's one more thing."

My stomach plunged. Of course there was a one more thing. Did I actually expect this guy to walk into my apartment and hand over almost half a million dollars? God, I was such an idiot. "What would that be, Mr. Evans?"

He pulled out a leather deposit bag. "Your mother gave Ms. Tuckerman fifty thousand dollars in cash. Told her that if something happened, she wanted to be sure Opa was taken care of. Opa couldn't convince her otherwise, so she eventually took it. We had been planning to hand it over to you when they were killed."

The missing fifty thousand. It had been Mama?

I was still in shock when he mentioned there were papers I had to sign. I could only nod.

For his part, Mr. Evans worked just as quick and efficiently as one would have expected a lawyer with David and Daniels to work. In no time, he guided me though a pile of papers, making certain I understood what each one said and pointing to every place I need to sign. My hand shook for the majority of the signing, but Mr. Evans was very kind and didn't bring it up at all.

He finally left with the signed papers and a promise to run them by the bank immediately. After that, he'd return to his office to finish the paperwork. He said he would request the money be transferred as soon as possible. But I had to admit, when I closed the door behind him, I wasn't sure I believed what had just happened.

CHAPTER TWENTY

*I*t had been two weeks since I'd left Mia's apartment. Two weeks and I'd managed not to send a text or leave a voicemail. However, my patience was wearing thin and it was only a matter of time before I did one or both.

When I'd left her apartment that day, my plan had been to give her time to think about us and how good we'd been together and how we'd only get better. Now, after two weeks? I was beginning to think I had vastly underestimated how much time she needed.

A horrible thought struck me. What if she'd moved and I didn't know? With her mother gone and her business closed, she might have decided to leave Boston altogether.

Fuck. Why hadn't I thought of that before today?

I looked at my watch and decided I'd leave the office as soon as possible and drive by her apartment to see if I spied her car in the parking lot. Unfortunately, I wouldn't be able to leave as early as I would have on any other day because I had a meeting starting soon.

As much as I wanted to drive by Mia's apartment, I'd be lying if I said I wasn't interested in seeing how this meeting went. The email had arrived a few days ago, the sender indicating an interest to meet with me about a potential partnership and signing off as M. Opa. I'd never heard of this Opa or of their company, but, I was interested.

Sara buzzed my phone ten minutes before the meeting was to start. "Mr. Butler, your two o'clock meeting is here."

Her voice sounded a bit off. I didn't say anything, though, right before I opened my mouth, I remembered hearing about her boyfriend breaking up with her. So, wisely, I simply replied, "Thank you. Please send them back to my office."

Within a few seconds, the sound of heels tapping down the hall could be heard. I felt like an ass, because I'd assumed I'd be meeting with a man. I listened as the steps grew closer and rose from my chair as they neared the door.

There was a quick knock and before I could answer, someone stepped inside.

It took me a few seconds to process that I knew who it was.

"Mia?" I asked, half in shock at seeing her in my office. Why was she here?

She smiled, but the left side of her mouth twitched a bit. It was the only noticeable indicator she felt even a tiny bit nervous. "I was afraid you'd turn down the meeting request if you knew it was me," she said. "Or even if you didn't, I was afraid you might not take me seriously. I thought it best this way."

It clicked at that moment that she was my meeting and I was so glad I kept to myself the question about what she was doing in my office. "I'll admit," I said as we moved toward the table in my office. "I was not expecting you at all."

Why had she requested a meeting to discuss being my partner? The last time I'd brought it up she'd shot me down almost before I had the words out of my mouth.

"Before we get down to business, I want to tell you something," she said and I wasn't sure if it was her tone of voice or the way she held herself, but there was something different about her. Something that made her look a lot more confident in herself. It was a very odd thought to have because, honestly, she'd never appeared to have lacked it before. But for some reason today, she could practically bottle it up and sell it.

Which is what she's doing now, you moron.

"Of course," I replied, while at the same time telling myself to pay attention to what she was saying and not to focus on how she looked, which was stunning in a smart looking light green suit, or to remember how she felt, or to try and guess if she was wearing garters. It took a lot of strength not to look under the table.

"I wanted to thank you for sending my contact information out to all those companies looking for consulting work."

"All what companies?" I asked because I had no idea what she was talking about.

Her smile faltered. "The companies that called me and needed me to work for them. Almost all of them mentioned my glowing recommendation."

I shook my head and her mouth formed an 'o' of surprise.

"But then how would they get a recommendation?" Her self-confidence slipped a notch and while I felt bad about that, I didn't want to lie to her. I refused to lie, no matter how uncomfortable it was. It was better than the alternative.

"I'm not sure, Mia." I sighed and decided it was time to confess. From this moment on, she would always get the entire story from me. "I'm glad to hear that you've had work the last few weeks, but I never would have called and recommended you to any of my competitors."

"You wouldn't?" she asked, sounding upset.

I hated the way she sounded and how quickly she changed away from the confident woman she'd been when she'd walked into my office.

"No." I smiled, but she still looked confused. "How could I convince you that you're miserable and unfulfilled unless you're working for me if you're perfectly content when you're working for someone else?"

"But if it wasn't you," she said, and I could almost see brain working through the possibilities. "Then who was it? It had to be someone."

I'd been considering who it could have been as soon as she mentioned someone had given recommendations from her job here. As difficult as it was to believe, there was only one possibility. "Piers," I said.

"No possible way." She shook her head. "He threatened me if I didn't take the deal he offered. No way would he give me a glowing recommendation."

"I can't imagine who else it could be." Truly, there was no one and I was shocked he'd done something nice for her.

"Let's find out for sure," she said. "Call him."

I raised an eyebrow. "You want me to pick up the phone and call him?"

"That is typically how it's done. I mean, feel free to use smoke signals, just know I'll need an interrupter." She spoke with a smile and the heaviness in my heart lifted.

"It's not that," I told her, knowing she probably wouldn't know my current relationship with Piers. "He might not answer my call. I haven't spoken to him since I fired him."

No, she didn't know. The look of surprise on her face told me that.

"You haven't?" she asked.

"I made it perfectly clear how serious I was to him." I shifted closer to her on the couch, just enough so I could feel her body heat. "Did you really think I was going to be able to overlook everything he did to you? Is that the type of man you think I am?"

She licked her lips and glanced down at her lap. "No."

Fuck, the sight of her tongue on her lips. But I pushed those thoughts from my head. It was enough for now that she didn't think badly of me. It didn't make the past go away. It didn't right our wrongs. But it was a start. I smiled. "Now let's get on with the meeting. You want to be my partner?"

And just like that, the self-assured and confident woman who'd walked through my door earlier was back. I don't even try to hide my joy.

I listened as she filled me on what had been going on and my excitement grew as she detailed her recent inheritance.

"That's wonderful news, Mia. Not that she passed away, but that because of her generosity, you don't have to worry about money like you were before."

"True," she admitted. "But it won't last forever and even if it did, I'm not one to sit around and do nothing. What I'd really like to do is be your business partner. If you're still thinking about having one," she said and I sensed a hint of hesitation.

My heart began to beat faster, but I told myself to slow down because we were a long way from any sort of agreement. "As you're aware, I was thinking about trying to find a partner. The business is getting to be too much to handle on my own. Especially with the Georgia expansion and definitely if I want to move forward with my plans for the international division. However, I was unable to find someone who met all my requirements. Until receiving your call, I had about given up on ever finding a partner."

"And now that you have had my call?" she asked.

I couldn't hope. I shouldn't hope. That's what I told myself anyway. Not that it did any good. Mia was in my office again. And she was talking about becoming my partner. How could I not hope? "I would very much like to become partners with you." I hadn't meant for it to come out in a whisper, but it did.

"What type of partner are you talking about exactly?" She tucked a piece of hair behind her ear and her fingers trembled ever so slightly.

She wasn't asking what I thought she was, was she?

There was no possible way. And yet, she had that look in her eye, the one that made anything seem possible. I started to hope again.

"What type of partner are you offering to be?" I asked, trying to match her nonchalant tone.

"You are such an ass," she said, in mock outrage.

"Good to know some things never change, isn't it?" When she didn't reply, I added, "I would like a work partner to stand with me and help me make our company the one that everyone talks about because it's so fucking good. Someone with experience, to challenge me and to motivate me and who I can do the same for."

She smiled and nodded. Her response made me bold.

I moved closer to her and stroked her cheek, sighing as she leaned into my touch. "And I want a partner outside of this office, who will build a life with me. Who knows that I'm an ass sometimes, but who wants me regardless. Someone I can love gently all night or fuck good and hard as the mood strikes us."

"Oh, yes," she said softly.

Encouraged by her positive responses, I took her hand and entwined out fingers. "I once thought it impossible for one person to fulfill both roles, but when I look at you, I feel that it could happen." I dropped my voice, "Is that what you were asking?" I somehow asked even with my heart in my throat.

"Yes," she managed to get out before I pressed my lips against hers.

For the last few weeks, I felt as if I'd been floating, drifting aimlessly from one task to another. Existing, but not really living. Or perhaps it was better described as if I'd been living in black and white. Her kiss made everything vibrant with color. It sounded ridiculous, even thinking it in my head, but that's what she did to me.

She made everything better. Simply by being her.

CHAPTER TWENTY-ONE

MIA

wo months later....

TENOR WALKED into my office with *that look* on his face. The one that said he wanted to do naughty things to me. Normally, I'd be down for anything he wanted, but not today, definitely not right now.

"Mia," he said, coming around the desk to me. "I have an idea."

I crossed my legs. "The last idea you had involved me naked against that glass window over there and almost got us slapped with an indecency charge."

The corner of his mouth quirked up. "That was

one of my better ideas, but you'll be pleased to know this idea has nothing to do with getting you naked. At least not until we get home."

'Home' for now was his massive townhouse in the city I'd recently moved into. We planned to get a place together, but hadn't got around to actually looking yet. For the moment, we were simply enjoying getting to know each other's quirks. The kind you only find out about after living together.

"I'm up to renegotiate clothing once we're home," I said. I loved living and working together. We really did fit together well. "What's your idea about then?"

"Are you still working on finding a date for that Italian gentleman moving to the States?"

"Yes," I replied, interested in where he was going.

Since my return to Bachelor International as a partner, we'd divided the day-to-day operations. I ran the Boston location, while Tenor managed the newly developed affiliate locations. We ran the international division together.

"Wren spent some time in Italy, didn't she?" he asked.

I templed my fingers. "Yes."

"Why don't we have her meet him for dinner that Saturday he's wanting a date for?"

Tenor didn't know about her history in Italy and I didn't feel as if it was my story to tell, so I only nodded and told him I'd think about it.

"I'm surprised you didn't think of her yourself," he said.

"It must have slipped my mind, you know, with all these ideas you keep having." I moved my chair closer to where he sat and brushed his thigh with my fingers.

He closed his eyes and hissed as I inched them higher. "Fuck, Mia. I'm trying really hard to wait until we get home."

I sat back and moved my hand. I'd just told him no and it wasn't nice to tease. "You're right. I'm sorry."

"No worries." He stood up and leaned over to give me a kiss, but I saw him eye the papers on my desk. "You've been talking with Piers?" he asked, showing he did care about the man, no matter what he might say.

Surprisingly enough, Piers was the one thing we still argued about. Though not over what anyone might guess about. I wanted Tenor to rehire him, and he didn't. We finally compromised by agreeing that if

Piers could find out what was going on with Benjamin Douglas and put a—legal—stop to him, he could return to his old position.

"Yes," I said. "Unfortunately, he's run into another dead end."

"Unfortunate for him maybe. I don't have a problem with that asshole not working here."

I laughed and he looked at me sharply. "Sorry," I said. "I was just thinking about a conversation I had with Wren a few months ago." Thinking back on those days made me stop and appreciate where I was now. I stood up. "I have an idea."

Tenor came to his feet beside me. "Does it involve either one of us naked and, or with a window?"

I took his tie and pulled him toward me. "It might." I gave him a quick kiss. "But you'll have to take me home first."

His took me in his arms. "God, I love you, woman."

"I love you, too. Now let's get out of here."

I didn't have to tell him twice.

Coming November 19, 2018

THE DATE DARE

I was six when Darcy Patrick moved next door.

By the time we were eight, we were best friends.

At fifteen, I gave a classmate a black eye for calling her names.

At sixteen, she talked me through asking my crush to prom.

I helped her get over her first heartbreak at nineteen.

Two years later, she returned the favor.

It wasn't until I was twenty-nine I realized I loved her.

And because I was too stupid to do anything about it,

at thirty, I lost her for good on a dare.

Darcy Patrick is tried of watching her best friend,

Elliott Taber, date the wrong kind of woman. When his latest flavor of the month walks out on him, she dares him to let her find his next date.

Elliott agrees, but only after Darcy agrees to allow him to do the same.

The dare is on.

The dates take place on the same night. One is an epic fail. The other is just plain epic.

Elliott isn't prepared for the onslaught of emotions hitting him as Darcy seemingly finds everything she ever wanted with the man he set her up with. He should be happy for her. He should leave her alone.

But he can't.

So he makes one more dare....

Keep reading for a sneak peek.

Darcy

Elliott and I have been best friends since Kindergarten, so I don't think it's a stretch to say I probably know him better than anyone. However, I have never been able to figure out why he dates the women he does.

Take for example the one he's with tonight. First of all, it's the World Series and Atlanta is playing. Elliott and I always watch the finals when they're in it. Granted, it's been years since they've made an appearance, but I knew it'd take more than a hot date to keep Elliott away from my place tonight.

It's fairly obvious his date, the second woman he's dated this October and henceforth referred to as O2, wasn't made aware of Elliott's plans prior their arrival. Not with the way she's leaning against the table examining her nails and the dagger of ice glare she shoots Elliott with every five minutes. Elliott is, of course, clueless. But that's Elliott for you.

He probably thinks the skintight dress she's wearing is fine for an evening of baseball and beer. More than likely, he's perfectly content to wait until after the game to peel the red fabric off of her, but O2 is not. She wants Elliott and she wants him *now*.

Not that anyone can blame her. I'll be the first in

line to admit Elliott is one of the best looking men I've ever seen. And thanks to his job as a trainer for the state's professional lacrosse team, the Georgia Storm, his body is pretty fantastic, too. Of course, I haven't seen him naked in ages.

Seven years, two months, five days, and about four hours, to be exact.

So yes, Elliott's a catch and a half and any woman would be proud to be on his arm. And yet, he keeps going out with these plastic lookalike women.

I skirt past O2 and sit on the couch beside him.

"O2's a little overdressed, isn't she?" I ask, reaching across him to grab a handful of chips.

"Her name is Alice," he says, keeping his eyes on the television.

"She makes it to November, she'll be Alice. Until then, she's O2."

"Don't let her hear you call her that. I don't feel like explaining your naming system to my date."

His voice is sharper than normal I look at him in shock. He's not actually serious about this one, is he?

"What crawled up your ass today?" I ask. I've been refusing to learn the names of his women for a least the last year and he's never minded. I turn my head to see what this latest one is up to and find she's chatting with, Richard, one of the players Elliott works with.

I actually end up watching her for a few minutes and not once does she ever turn her head toward Elliott. She's completely caught up in her conversation with Richard. At one point he says something and she laughs this horrible sounding laugh that is part hyena and part strangled cat.

Then, right there in my kitchen with God and half the Storm players present, she reaches out a perfectly manicured nail and runs it down the guy's chest. Now I've never mastered fine art of lip reading, but I'm pretty good at interpreting body language and her body wasn't so much saying *You must excuse me so I can go sit with my date* but rather, *Let's blow this joint so I can blow you.*

I'm not sure if Richard knows she came with Elliot. I'd like to think not. In the Utopia I've created in my brain, work friends do not walk around with their hand on your date's ass. But then again, I work in the hotel industry and Elliott works with professional athletes. I know from previous conversations with him that a few members of the team are into some pretty kinky shit, so I don't know, maybe they do.

But when I glance back at Elliot, he's watching

them with a look that is so raw and vulnerable that I swallow the smart ass comment I was about to say and put my hand on his knee.

"You deserve better, Elliott Taber," I whisper, so no one hears, but the game is back on following a commercial break and no one is paying us any attention.

He shakes his head and looks surprised for a few seconds. It's almost as if he'd been asleep and I woke him up.

"What?" he asks.

I nod to the corner of the kitchen where Richard and O2 are trying to make out without looking like they're making out. Which really means they're standing in the corner of my kitchen and being all handsy when they think no one's watching.

"I was just saying you deserve better than O2 over there. I mean, really? What's she doing hanging all over Richard when she came here with you?" I suddenly can't stand looking at them anymore so I turn back to face Elliott. "She's a guest in my house. I have a good mind to kick her out."

"Don't worry about it. I'm not," he says and he actually doesn't look upset or put off in anyway.

I can't get over how calm he's acting. Seriously, this is not normal and all at once I'm growing more and more concerned about his state of mind. How can he calmly sit there like it's nothing while his date is all but climbing over another man who also happens to be his work associate?

"You're entirely too calm about this," I tell him. "It's not normal."

He sighs deeply right as a chorus of cheers go up around us and we both realize we're missing a good part of the game. When everything calms back down, he leans over to me.

"We don't have a normal relationship," he says in a low voice.

"What do you mean by that?" I ask. "How many people do you know that have been friends for twenty-five years?"

His gaze is steady. "I wasn't talking about me and you."

"Then who were you talking about?"

Another cheer goes up and Elliott brushes me off. "We'll talk about it later. Come on and let's watch the rest of the game."

Our conversation isn't finished and he knows this. But I agree that this isn't the best place or time to talk. Besides, if he wasn't talking about our relationship, then he had to have been talking about him and O2. And if there was any relationship I don't want to talk about while my boys win the World Series, it's that one.

For the next few hours, we fall back into our old and comfortable routine of yelling at the players and the umpires. We eat way too much, drink way too much, and laugh way too loud. In other words, good times.

When the game ends and people begin to leave, I look around and both O2 and Richard are gone. Elliott shrugs like it's no big deal, but I'm not going to let him get away with it that easily.

As it so happens, I'll be staying in Atlanta for an extended period of time. Typically, with my job as a brand expert with an international hotel chain, I'm only in my home city for two weeks out of the month. Since the season has just ended for the Storm, Elliott will be around as well. It'll be the perfect occasion for me to finally get to the bottom of what the hell his problem is with women.

"Looks like O2 left your sorry ass," I say with a punch to his arm when everyone has left other than him.

"*Alice* and I have an understanding." His smile is back in place and I can't tell if he's putting on a mask or not.

I can't imagine any couple with any sort of relationship that finds it acceptable for one person to leave the other in the middle of an evening out, but whatever. He can attempt to explain it to me later.

"You and me," I tell him. "Tomorrow night. The Barn. Seven o'clock. O2 isn't invited and you best not even think of bringing O3." It's our favorite steak house and he wouldn't dream about not showing up.

He jokes arounds, but eventually agrees. Before he leaves to catch the cab he called, he leans over and kisses my cheek goodnight. It's something he's done countless times, but in the second before he pulls away, I notice a hint of hesitation. He's gone and out the door before I realize I'm standing in my doorway with my hand on my cheek, lightly touching the place his lips had been seconds before.

Want more? Preorder here: https://amzn.to/2CbTDWD

COMING IN JANUARY 2019

ROMAN ROUGE
Bachelor International, Book 2

Wren Prescott was born to dance. Unfortunately, her dancing career died prematurely years ago on the Italian slopes as a result of a drunken dare she regrets everyday. But it wasn't just her career she lost, but also the only man she'd ever loved. He was a loss that hurt so badly, she never even told her best friend, Mia about him.

Fashion designer Luca Botticelli is a success in every way except one: love. Recently located to the US, he's ready to leave his mark on American fashion with his latest line, created as a goodbye to his dancing bird, the beautiful ballerina who stole his heart years ago and left without saying a word. He puts his love life in the hands of Tenor Butler, but isn't expecting much.

When Wren and Luca's paths cross unexpectedly, neither of them are ready for the rush of emotions that follow. They both want closure, but first they have to face the demons of their past. And in doing so, they'll have to determine if their love story is the genuine article or a horrid fraud.

DETAILS COMING SOON!

RACK ACADEMY SERIES:

Master Professor

Headmaster

BACHELOR INTERNATIONAL:

American Asshole

Writing as Tara Thomas

Shattered Fear*

Hidden Fate*

Twisted End*

Darkest Night

Deadly Secret

Broken Promise

*eNovella

ABOUT THE AUTHOR

Want to stay up to date on my releases and deals? Sign up for my newsletter here.

Even though she graduated with a degree in science, Tara knew she'd never be happy doing anything other than writing. Specifically, writing love stories.

She started with a racy BDSM story and found she was not quite prepared for the unforeseen impact it would have. Nonetheless, she continued and The

Submissive Series novels would go on to be both New York Times and USA Today Bestsellers. One of those, THE MASTER, was a 2017 RITA finalist for Best Erotic Romance.

Now she is focusing on new contemporary romances that allow her the freedom to write and publish on her own schedule.

Made in the USA
Middletown, DE
12 September 2018